NET BANDITS

Rob looked at the blank e-mail page. That was it! He might not be able to run for help – but then perhaps he didn't need to.

Quickly, he flicked on the CAPS LOCK key and began to type . . .

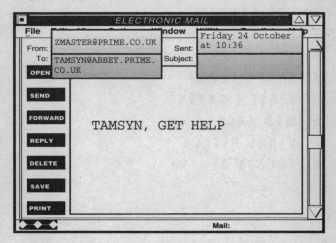

But no sooner had he started than he heard Elaine clattering back towards his room.

Rob's mind was in a whirl. What was he going to do? The most he had time for was . . . yes, it could work.

Rob's fingers hammered at the RETURN key. Then, as he heard the scrape of the key turning in his door lock, he frantically typed some more characters.

Desperately, he flicked the mouse onto the SEND button and clicked once.

He was just in ti

Titles in the

▽ INTERNET DETECTIVES

series

1. NET BANDITS
2. ESCAPE KEY
3. SPEED SURF
4. CYBER FEUD
5. SYSTEM CRASH
6. WEB TRAP
7. VIRUS ATTACK
8. ACCESS DENIED

INTERNET DETECTIVES

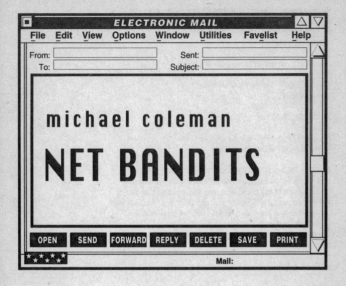

michael coleman

NET BANDITS

A WORKING PARTNERS BOOK

MACMILLAN CHILDREN'S BOOKS

First published 1996 by Macmillan Children's Books
a division of Macmillan Publishers Limited
25 Eccleston Place, London SW1W 9NF
and Basingstoke

Associated companies throughout the world

Created by Working Partners Limited
London W6 0HE

ISBN 0 330 34734 9

Copyright © Working Partners Limited 1996
Computer graphics by Jason Levy

9 8 7 6 5 4 3 2

A CIP catalogue record for this book is available from
the British Library.

Printed by Mackays of Chatham plc, Kent

For Brian Bloor, with many thanks

CHAPTER 1

Portsmouth, England.
Thursday 16th October, 8.30 a.m.

Rob Zanelli leaned forward and pressed the button on the front of his computer. Instantly, the soft whirr of the computer's hard disk started up. Moments later his display screen was scrolling up lines of information as the computer worked through the opening sequence Rob had defined for it.

He didn't bother to watch. Instead, he gazed out of his bedroom window at the broad expanse of garden at the front of the Zanellis' large house. They lived in Portsmouth, in Manor House, occupying a proud position high up on Portsdown Hill.

From here, the whole town looked as if it was laid out like a carpet. Tall glass tower blocks jutted up from the rows of red-roofed houses stretching away into the distance. Over to his right, Rob could see the glistening waters of Portsmouth Harbour. He watched for a moment as a grey Royal Navy destroyer nosed its way into the dockyard.

Then, as the screen display switched on, Rob turned back to it.

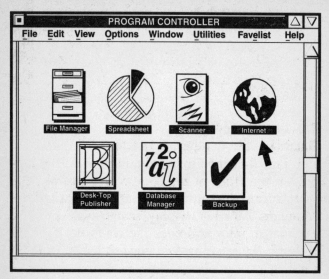

He reached to his left and swept the computer's mouse to one side. On the screen an arrow-shaped pointer moved onto the Internet icon – a miniature globe. Rob gave the mouse's left button a sharp click.

As he did so he looked up, to one of the shelves above his computer desk. Next to a row of manuals sat a small black box, a row of red lights flickering madly on its front. Two cables led from the box. One of them connected to the back of his computer. The other snaked away to a telephone socket in the corner of the room.

The black box was a modem, a gadget for enabling his computer to connect to other computers as though they were talking to each other on the telephone.

As the red lights settled into a fixed pattern, the screen display went dark. For those few moments Rob's face was reflected in the screen, a typical thirteen-year-old's face with bright alert eyes and wavy brown hair.

And then his reflection was gone. As the display lit up once more, Rob moved closer to the computer. However many times he did this part, it still amazed him. Suddenly – there it was.

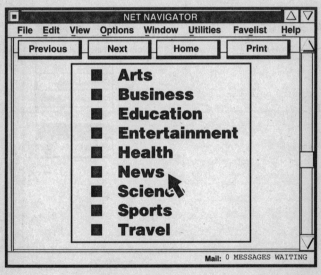

He was connected to the Internet, a network of computers which covered the whole world. From his keyboard now he could send a message anywhere: America . . . Australia . . . Canada . . . Papua New Guinea – anywhere with a computer that was connected to the Net.

He sat for a moment, thinking about what to do first. Where to go? Then, he made a decision – and smiled to himself.

With all the world to choose from, he'd decided to have a look at what was going on in . . . Portsmouth, the city he'd lived in all his life.

He moved the pointer up to the menu bar, and clicked on the word FaveList. A second menu dropped down, containing the locations on the Net that Rob most regularly visited:

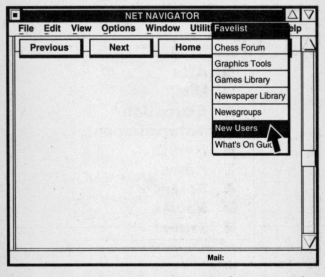

He clicked on 'New Users'. There was the faintest of pauses before the computer responded. Rob scanned the list on the screen quickly, his eyes flicking down the row of names with practised ease. As he saw one, he smiled.

'Hey,' he said. 'A school Newbie.'

A Newbie was any newcomer to the Internet, and the command Rob had clicked had been to ask for a list of all new joiners in his area over the past month. There, in the middle of the list, one name had caught his attention.

'Abbey School', read the line. Moving the mouse pointer up to the line, Rob clicked again. At once, another page flashed up onto the screen.

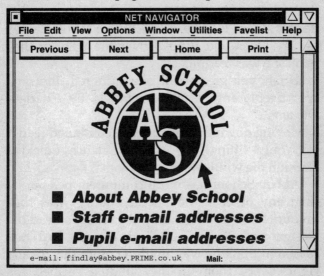

Rob checked out each option in turn, nodding slowly as he did so. Only one user so far, and that was a member of staff. No point sending messages there. Still, things might change. Rob made a mental note to keep on checking the Abbey School home page for new user IDs. Sooner or later, he hoped, they'd actually let some of the kids use the Internet.

'Then I'll have me some fun,' he said to himself.

Abbey School, Portsmouth.
Thursday 16th October, 8.45 a.m.

In one movement, Tamsyn Smith brushed a hand through her short, dark hair, pushed through the double doors leading into Abbey School's technology block and flipped over the page of the book she was reading.

'Uriah, you greaseball!' she muttered. Tamsyn was deeply into *David Copperfield* by Charles Dickens.

Moving down the corridor she continued reading, only lifting her eyes to glance quickly through the windows of each room.

'Abbey School has more computers per pupil than any other school in the county,' was the favourite line of Mr Findlay, the school's head of Design and Technology, and Tamsyn had no reason to think he was anything other than dead right. Every room in the building seemed to be jammed full of the things.

Not only that. A decent number of them were already turned on, each with someone in a distinctive maroon Abbey sweatshirt sitting in front of its screen – even at this time of the morning, before registration!

What is it about computers? thought Tamsyn.

She enjoyed using them – but not every minute of the day! Why was it that some kids couldn't get enough of them? Even kids like Josh who she'd known ever since primary school and who, in every other way, was perfectly normal – well, as normal as any boy *could* be.

Marking her place and tucking her book into her shoulder bag, Tamsyn headed for the room at the very end of the corridor. *Still*, she thought, *at least I don't have to waste time looking for Josh. I always know where to find him!*

The door was labelled COMPUTER CLUB in psychedelic colours. This was actually a regular school laboratory, but one which could be used at certain times of the day only by members of the Computer Club. Through the window Tamsyn could see Josh sitting inside, staring intently at a screen. She bustled in.

'Hang on, hang on,' Josh said before she could even get a word out. 'I'm at level seven and going *brilliantly!*'

Tamsyn flopped into a chair, waving her hand in the air. 'Fine. Don't mind me, Josh. I've got *all day!*'

Josh showed no signs of minding. He didn't give Tamsyn a second glance as his fingers flashed across the keyboard and what looked like a totally chaotic gang of red marauders charged around the screen.

Finally, with a cry of anguish, Josh slumped back in his chair.

'Got me,' he moaned. 'Zapped by the Dark Destroyer!'

'Aaah,' cooed Tamsyn, patting him on the shoulder. 'Never mind, Josh. Better luck next time. Can I speak now? Is that OK?'

Josh swung round in his seat and grinned. He was a big boy for his age and his sweatshirt looked a size too small for him. Above his cheerful face was a shock of dark hair which Tamsyn had only ever seen combed for the benefit of the school photographer.

'Permission granted,' he laughed. 'Speak on.'

'Have you done the French homework?' asked Tamsyn. 'I couldn't understand a word of it.'

'All Greek to you, is it?' laughed Josh.

Tamsyn tried to glare at him. 'Well, have you?' she said.

Mais oui,' said Josh. 'I have.'

'How?' said Tamsyn, shaking her head. She just couldn't understand how Josh always managed to do the homework when, in class, he seemed as hopeless at French as she was. 'Oh, it doesn't matter. Just show me, so that I don't look a complete dumbhead when Mam'selle Pirri asks me something.'

'Tell you what – I can show you,' said Josh.

'What?'

'Where to find the French Department's new CD-ROM,' laughed Josh. 'How do you think I sussed it all out?'

'Josh. Just show me the answers, eh?'

'OK,' said Josh. 'Later. All right?'

Even as he'd been talking to Tamsyn, Josh had been inching round in his chair.

On the screen in front of him a three-dimensional view of a castle's ramparts had been overlaid by a box carrying the message:

Josh tapped quickly at the 'Y' key.

'Jo-osh!' Tamsyn groaned as the computer sprang into life once more. 'It's French straight after break!'

'See you at break, then,' said Josh. 'I want one more go at this. While I'm warmed up.'

As the computer finished its sinister introductory tune, Josh hunched low over the keyboard.

Tamsyn stood up. 'You could play that at break, you know!'

Josh didn't answer. Fingers darting from one key to another, he had eyes only for the flashing figures on the screen in front of him.

Tamsyn pushed her chair back with a clonk. She snatched up her school bag. She rattled open the door. Josh didn't look up.

Computer games! thought Tamsyn angrily. The only way you could attract Josh's attention was to stick a pin in him, or turn off the electricity.

Turn off the electricity . . .

As she stood at the door, Tamsyn saw the switch on the wall. She couldn't resist it.

With a swiftness of touch that Josh would have been proud of, she flicked the switch to OFF. Then she shot out of the door and down the corridor, hooting with laughter.

By the time Josh's shout of 'Tamsyn! I'll get you for that!' reached her she was at the double doors and on her way out of the Technology Block.

Abbey School.
Thursday 16th October, 2.50 p.m.
Mr Findlay made his announcement at the end of their Design and Technology lesson, the final period of the day.

'One more thing before you go,' he said, raising his voice above the feet-shuffling and book-closing that signalled the end of every lesson. 'I thought you'd like to know that Abbey School is now linked to the information super-highway.'

'You mean,' cried Josh at once, 'the school's got an Internet link?'

Mr Findlay removed his spectacles and began

polishing them on his tie. 'That is exactly what I do mean, Josh. You've used the Internet before, have you?'

'No,' said Josh, 'but I've read all about it!'

Sitting two rows back, Tamsyn raised her eyebrows. *Read* all about it?

'You can send messages and stuff to anybody who's connected. And there's all sort of programs you can get hold of,' Josh went on excitedly. 'Loads of stuff. Games and . . . well, games and more games!'

'Rather more than games, I believe,' smiled Mr Findlay. 'But we won't know how the school can best use this new facility until we really explore what's out there—'

'Surf the Net, Mr Findlay,' interrupted Josh. 'That's what it's called when you check out what's on other computers.'

Mr Findlay nodded. 'Indeed it is, Josh.' He picked up a thick manual from the desk at his side. 'So, what I'm looking for is a couple of enthusiastic surfers . . .'

A forest of hands immediately shot up.

'. . . to spend some of their *own* time . . .'

Hands immediately went down again as a large proportion of the forest was felled as quickly as it had sprung up.

'. . . to use the Internet link and write a report on how valuable it might be for the school.'

As the words 'write' and 'report' were uttered, a few more hands dropped. One hand, though, was still reaching high, a towering pine in the middle of a scattering of saplings. The hand belonged to Josh.

'Josh Allan, then,' said Mr Findlay. He looked at Josh. 'Not much doubt that you'll find plenty to say about the link.'

'No, sir!' said Josh. He couldn't wait to get started.

Mr Findlay was still looking about the room, though. 'But I think you might only see the good things, Josh. And I'd quite like to have somebody else look for the disadvantages. Somebody who's perhaps not so keen. Any volunteers?'

For a good few seconds, not a muscle moved. Then, slowly, a hand went up.

'Tamsyn!' cried Mr Findlay. 'Thank you for volunteering! I'm sure you and Josh will produce an excellent report!'

CHAPTER 2

Tamsyn's house.
Tuesday 21st October, 7.45 p.m.

'Tamsyn! Telephone!'

Up in her room, Tamsyn buried her head and *David Copperfield* under her pillow. It didn't help. Moments later her door was flung open by her young brother, Nick.

'You deaf or what?' he yelled at the top of his voice. 'It's the telephone. For you-hoo!'

'Who is it?'

'Who do you think it is?' said Nick. 'Josh.'

Tamsyn groaned. Why had she done it? Why?

When Mr Findlay had asked for a second volunteer it had seemed like a good idea to put her hand up. She'd still been steaming about Josh and it had seemed the perfect way of showing him that computers weren't just about playing games.

But it hadn't seemed like a good idea for long. By the time the bell had gone and the lesson was over she was already having second thoughts. And by the time Josh collared her outside the Technology Block, it had turned into a very *bad* idea.

Josh had held up the thick manual Mr Findlay

had given him. 'Look at this lot! I'm glad I'm not doing it on my own. So, when we going to start? How about tomorrow, after school?'

'Tomorrow? As soon as that?'

'Yeah. Just for a couple of hours.'

'On a Friday?' she'd exclaimed. 'No chance, Josh. Fridays I get my homework done, then catch up on all the soaps on telly.'

'How about today, then?' Josh had asked on Monday.

A shake of the head. 'No chance. Hockey practice. No, today's out.'

'When, then? Tomorrow?'

'Tuesday . . . Tuesday . . . what do I do on a Tuesday?' On the spur of the moment she'd been unable to think of anything – anything other than the fact that she'd almost certainly got something she wanted to do more than sit next to Josh while he scanned the Internet for computer games.

'Could be,' she'd stalled. 'Ask me tomorrow.'

But Josh hadn't asked her that day, because he hadn't had a chance to get near enough. Tamsyn had deliberately ducked out of classrooms almost as soon as the bell had gone and spent large amounts of time in the girls' cloakrooms. She was down to the last hundred pages of *David Copperfield* and *that* was how she planned to spend her Tuesday evening – by reading the rest and finding out how evil Uriah Heep got it in the end.

'Nick!' whispered Tamsyn. 'Tell him I'm not in. Tell him I've gone to my piano lesson.'

'Ooh, I couldn't do that,' her brother said over his shoulder. 'We haven't got a piano.'

'Then, tell him . . . I don't know,' exploded Tamsyn, 'tell him I've got bubonic plague. Tell him they've just carried me out on a stretcher. Tell him anything!'

She glanced at the copy of *A Tale of Two Cities*, another Dickens book, sitting on her bedside table. She really didn't want to be playing games tomorrow night either.

Nick went down the stairs. She heard him mutter something softly into the telephone. Moments later, he was back upstairs again.

'I just told him something,' he said.

'Well done,' said Tamsyn. 'What did you tell him?'

'I told him you're here, and you won't be a minute, so he shouldn't hang up whatever he does.'

'You lousy toad!' screeched Tamsyn.

'Croak, croak,' said Nick. 'Now get a move on.' With a sigh, Tamsyn shuffled downstairs. *A Tale of Two Cities* was going to have to wait.

'Hello, Josh,' she said brightly. 'Tomorrow, after school? Right, you're on.'

Abbey School.
Wednesday 22nd October, 3.30 p.m.
Josh pointed at the glowing computer screen.

'This is how it looks when you're connected to the Net,' he said. 'Think of it as a menu in a restaurant. All you have to do is to choose what you want to do.'

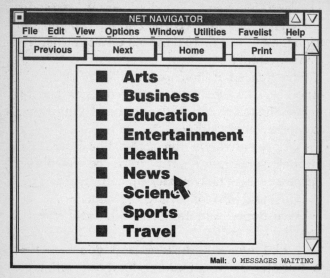

Tamsyn scanned the list. 'How about if you don't want to do anything?' she said.

'You choose FILE and QUIT,' said Josh. 'Then you toddle straight off to Mr Findlay and say you've changed your mind, you don't want to do it after all and you've left me to do it all on my own . . .'

Tamsyn held up her hands. 'Joke, Josh! Come on, let's get stuck into it. Which one do you want me to pick? ENTERTAINMENT?'

Josh shook his head. He pointed at the bottom line. 'Electronic mail,' he said. 'Let's have a go at sending some messages.'

Tamsyn clicked on the word 'Mail', as Josh pointed. The display changed immediately.

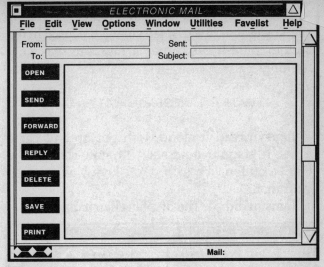

'Hey, where are you going?' said Tamsyn as Josh got up and went across to sit at another computer on the other side of the room.

Josh swung the display round for Tamsyn to see. He had exactly the same picture on the screen of his computer.

'One I prepared a little earlier,' he grinned. 'This one is connected to the Internet as well.' He began typing.

'Now what are you doing?' said Tamsyn, starting to get up.

'Wait there. You'll see.' Josh typed in some more, then ended with a flourish. Finally he slid his mouse across and clicked the left-hand button. 'Right,' he called across to Tamsyn. 'Anything changed on your screen?'

Tamsyn looked. 'Nothing,' she said.

But no sooner had she said it than, with a little beeping sound, the display changed. Down in the bottom right-hand corner a message was now flashing.

MAIL: 1 MESSAGE WAITING

Tamsyn read it aloud. Josh got up and came across to stand behind her. 'OK, now click on the OPEN button,' he said. 'You know, as in open your mail?'

Tamsyn did so. The display changed again.

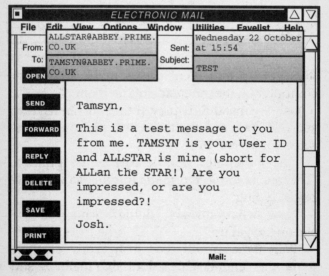

'Impressed?' said Tamsyn. 'By getting a message from the other side of the room?'

'But I *could* have been on the other side of the world!' cried Josh. 'That's the whole point. It's just as easy to send a message anywhere. Anywhere at all.'

Tamsyn nodded. It *was* impressive. But was it useful?

'Go on, then.' It was Josh, nudging her from behind.

'Go on what?'

'Reply. Send me a message back. Click on the REPLY button,' said Josh, leaning over and pointing at the screen. Tamsyn did as she was told, slightly irritated that she had to be told, but interested to see what would happen next. As she clicked on the REPLY button the screen simply scrolled Josh's message down so that Tamsyn could type in something herself.

```
Thank you for your interesting
message, Josh. Not exactly
'David Copperfield', but pretty
good for you!
```

As she finished, Tamsyn clicked on SEND. Moments later a blip sounded from Josh's computer.

'There you go,' said Josh. 'It's arrived in my mailbox. And it'll stay there until I look at it. Good, eh?'

Tamsyn laughed. Josh was like a kid with a new toy. 'Josh, it's good. But I'll take a book any day.'

With a big grin on his face, Josh sat down next to her. 'So it's a good book you want, is it? Right, watch this.'

Quickly he returned to the opening menu. This time he clicked on ARTS.

'Think of this as digging deeper and deeper into a mound of information,' said Josh as yet another menu came up, this one full of text with some words underlined. He clicked on a line reading 'A Catalogue of Electronic Texts on the Internet'. This time, a list of book titles came on the screen. Tamsyn had just enough time to realize that she was looking at a list of classics before Josh clicked again. Within ten seconds, no more, up onto the screen came a page of text.

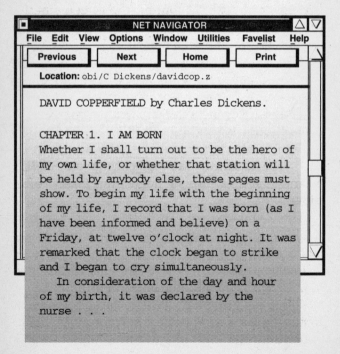

NET NAVIGATOR

File   Edit   View   Options   Window   Utilities   Favelist   Help

| Previous | Next | Home | Print |

Location: obi/C Dickens/davidcop.z

DAVID COPPERFIELD by Charles Dickens.

CHAPTER 1. I AM BORN
Whether I shall turn out to be the hero of my own life, or whether that station will be held by anybody else, these pages must show. To begin my life with the beginning of my life, I record that I was born (as I have been informed and believe) on a Friday, at twelve o'clock at night. It was remarked that the clock began to strike and I began to cry simultaneously.

In consideration of the day and hour of my birth, it was declared by the nurse . . .

'But – that's . . .' began Tamsyn.

'David Copperfield,' laughed Josh. 'Every page of it if you care to scroll through it!'

Tamsyn looked at him. 'Where did it come from?'

'Would you believe a computer in America? I came across it by accident when I was messing about – when you were catching up with all your soaps, I think it was.'

Tamsyn smiled. 'OK, Josh. I'm sorry I gave you a hard time. I thought you'd just want to play games and nothing else . . .'

Josh's eyes lit up. 'Funny you should mention games. I've found stacks of 'em! Let me show you.'

It was the cue for Tamsyn to pick up her bag and sling it over her shoulder. 'Let's make that lesson two, eh? Tomorrow.'

'You're on,' said Josh. He looked at his watch. 'Crikey, is that the time?'

Tamsyn looked at her own watch. It was much later than she'd thought. Could that be why people like Josh spent so long with computers – because they simply lost track of time?

Josh was on his feet, scrambling to get his things together. 'I'm not supposed to be here! I'm supposed to be picking up some shopping on the way home!'

Tamsyn put her bag down again. 'Go on, then. I'll finish off in here.'

'Don't forget to turn the computers off,' said Josh, cramming his books and papers into a holdall that already looked as though it was holding all it could take. 'Mr Findlay goes spare if he finds them left on.'

'Don't worry,' said Tamsyn. 'Turning computers off is my speciality, remember!'

Josh charged down the Technology Block corridor and out through the swing doors like a whirlwind. Slowly, Tamsyn walked over to the computer Josh had been using, feeling the gentle heat coming from the back of it.

She closed down the application to return to the opening menu. Selecting the exit option, she waited until the system had closed itself down before turning off the control unit.

As the computer's fan slowed to a halt, the room seemed quiet. Quieter, anyway, with only the computer she'd been using still on.

And so it was that she heard, quite distinctly, the little beep which told her that an electronic mail message had arrived.

Manor House. 5.30 p.m.

Rob Zanelli looked round as he heard the gentle knock at the door of his room.

'Hi, Dad,' Rob said as his father came in.

Mr Zanelli was smartly dressed in a blue business suit. His dark hair was flecked with grey at his temples.

'Hi,' said Mr Zanelli. 'How's things?'

Rob shrugged. 'Fine, I guess.'

Mr Zanelli sat down on Rob's bed. He nodded

towards Rob's school books, neatly stacked on his desk. 'Work going well? How's Elaine? Knocking you into shape?' He laughed, but not very convincingly.

Rob sighed. He seemed to have had this same conversation with his father so often before.

'She's OK, Dad. But you know what I want.'

It was Mr Zanelli's turn to sigh. He was the managing director of his own company, *GAME-ZONE*, which produced computer games. Mrs Zanelli was a director of the company, too. Between them they earned a lot of money. But they both knew – as did Rob – that there was one thing that all their money couldn't buy for them.

'Rob,' said Mr Zanelli. 'I know what you're going to say. You want to go to school. Right?'

Rob nodded. 'Of course. And I can't see why you won't let me.'

'You *know* why. Because we're frightened for you.'

'But I'm not. Why should you be?'

Mr Zanelli stood up abruptly. 'Look. Let's discuss this another time, eh?'

Rob nodded. Discuss it another time – it was the answer he always got. And nothing would change. He'd still not be allowed to go to school with other kids, still have to be tutored at home, on his own, by people like Elaine Kirk.

'What's buzzing on the Internet?' said Mr Zanelli, seizing the opportunity to change the subject. 'Made any new contacts?'

'A few,' said Rob, brightening slightly. His

parents might not be prepared to let him go to school with other kids, but they certainly tried to make up for it with what they provided. He had every bit of computer kit worth having, and then some more.

'Where?' said Mr Zanelli. 'Which continent – or are they in all of them?'

Rob gave him a smile. 'This continent, actually. This city.'

'Portsmouth?'

'A Newbie site. They've just joined the Net. I've been waiting for them to set up some User IDs.'

'And have they?'

Rob grinned. 'A couple. I found them just before you came in. In fact I've just sent an e-mail to one of them . . .'

Abbey School. 5.34 p.m.

Tamsyn stared at the screen and its flashing message.

```
MAIL: 1 MESSAGE WAITING
```

Had the thing gone wrong? Had she broken it just by looking at it? No, of course she hadn't. She knew what had happened. Somebody had just sent her a message.

But who?

The answer came to her at once. Who else? Josh, of course. The shopping business had just been an excuse to get away. He must have gone off to some other computer he knew about in the school and logged on to the Internet from there. The library, probably.

Typical! thought Tamsyn. Still, she might as well join in. With a shake of her head, she sat down and clicked on OPEN – and saw at once that whoever the message was from, it wasn't from Josh.

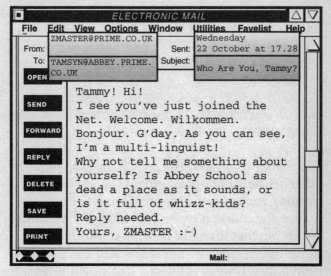

'ZMASTER?' snorted Tamsyn. 'Sounds like a weirdo magician.'

Even so, it was a bit eerie. How had this ZMASTER, whoever-he-was, found out about her? Had he been spying on them in some way she didn't understand? She didn't know whether to encourage him by replying – or simply to delete his message.

I'll answer, she decided. If nothing else, the fact that she'd received an e-mail from somebody outside school would make Josh green with envy! Tentatively, she clicked on the REPLY icon and started typing:

```
ZMASTER, EH? WHAT A FUNNY NAME!
NO, ABBEY SCHOOL ISN'T TOTALLY
DEAD, AND IT ISN'T TOTALLY FULL
OF WHIZZ-KIDS EITHER.
WHAT IT DOES HAVE ARE LOTS OF
PEOPLE WITH NORMAL NAMES,
THOUGH!
SO - WHAT'S YOUR NAME, ZMASTER?!
P.S. MY NAME IS TAMSYN, NOT
'TAMMY'!
```

I wonder what he'll make of that? Tamsyn thought after sending her note. Perhaps there'd be a reply waiting for her in the morning?

But she didn't have to wait until the morning. Thinking that it would be a good idea to start on their Internet report while she had the information at hand, she left the computer on and began to jot down some notes. It blipped before she'd finished.

'Already?' muttered Tamsyn, as she saw the flashing MAIL WAITING once again.

Moments later, she was glaring at the screen.

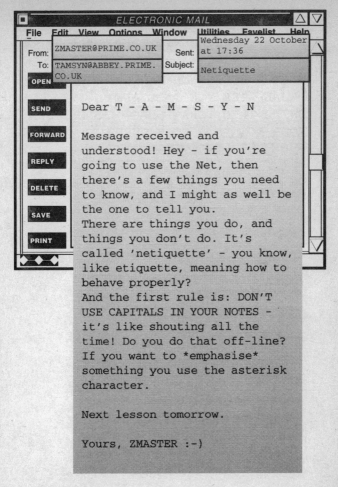

File Edit View Options Window Utilities Favelist Help

From: ZMASTER@PRIME.CO.UK
To: TAMSYN@ABBEY.PRIME.CO.UK

Sent: Wednesday 22 October at 17:36
Subject: Netiquette

Dear T - A - M - S - Y - N

Message received and understood! Hey - if you're going to use the Net, then there's a few things you need to know, and I might as well be the one to tell you.
There are things you do, and things you don't do. It's called 'netiquette' - you know, like etiquette, meaning how to behave properly?
And the first rule is: DON'T USE CAPITALS IN YOUR NOTES - it's like shouting all the time! Do you do that off-line? If you want to *emphasise* something you use the asterisk character.

Next lesson tomorrow.

Yours, ZMASTER :-)

Tamsyn muttered as she glared.

'Netiquette? Don't use capitals?' She felt her top lip curling angrily. 'Who does he think he is?'

'Right, ZMASTER,' she muttered as she began typing, 'see what you make of this!'

GET THIS ZMASTER, WHOEVER YOU
ARE, I'M USING CAPITALS HERE
BECAUSE I *AM* SHOUTING! WHEN I
WANT A LESSON ON MANNERS FROM A
PRUNE LIKE YOU I'LL ASK!
UNTIL THEN, CRAWL BACK UNDER
YOUR ROCK AND STAY THERE!!!

CHAPTER 3

Manor House. Thursday 23 October, 9.05 a.m.

'Rob, did Elaine say she was going to be late this morning?'

Rob looked up as his mother came into his room. She was dressed in her smartest suit. There must be a big meeting going on at *GAMEZONE* that morning.

'No,' said Rob. He checked the clock on his wall. 'Anyhow, she's hardly late, Mum. It's only just after nine.'

'I have some papers to go over,' said Mrs Zanelli. 'We have a board meeting at ten o'clock.'

Mrs Zanelli smiled, but didn't move. Instead, she paced over to the window and looked out. There was no sign of Elaine Kirk's tired-looking car.

'If I went to school like other kids . . .' began Rob.

'You wouldn't need a private tutor and I wouldn't be waiting for her to arrive,' Mrs Zanelli said sharply, but with a hint of a smile. 'Right?'

'Pretty close,' said Rob.

His mother knelt close by his chair. Rob could smell her most expensive perfume. It had to be a *really* big meeting that morning!

'Rob, your father and I talked about this again last evening. We know how much you want to . . .' She paused, as if she was looking for the right words. '. . . to be treated like other kids your age. But we're not ready for that. Not yet. Understand?'

Rob wanted to say, no, he didn't understand. He wanted to say he thought she and his father were thinking more about themselves than they were about him. But he couldn't.

In the end, he just nodded. 'Sure. But don't think I'm going to stop nagging you.'

'Oh, we don't think that,' said Mrs Zanelli, standing up and heading for the window again. 'Not at all.'

A harsh-sounding buzzer interrupted them. Mrs Zanelli pulled back the curtains and looked out once more. This time, a car was standing at the side of Manor House's winding tarmac driveway. 'Oh, good. Here she is. Can you open the door for her while I get my case?'

Rob moved over to a silver panel on the wall near the door. The panel had a small grille and two buttons. Rob punched the left-hand button. 'Friend or foe?' he said irritably.

'It's Elaine, Rob,' crackled a voice through the grille.

'How do I know?' said Rob.

'Rob, stop playing about and let her in!'

Mrs Zanelli shouted from the hallway.

Rob punched the right-hand button. Immediately he heard a muffled buzz sound from the hallway as the security lock on the heavy front door snapped open.

There was the briefest of conversations in the hall before Mrs Zanelli departed with a shout of 'Bye!'

Rob gathered his books together and set off down the hallway. Manor House was old and roomy, with an impressive square entrance hall. One of its many doors led into the comfortable lounge. This was the room in which he had his lessons.

Elaine Kirk was already unpacking her black briefcase. She was a small woman with sharp features and a hairdo that looked as though it could be cut with a knife. As usual, Rob noticed, she was dressed immaculately.

She was Rob's fourth tutor, the previous three having left for one reason or another over the years he'd been having lessons at home. All had said much the same thing to Mr and Mrs Zanelli in their letters of resignation: that Rob was a very intelligent boy, and that he could undoubtedly do better if he'd put as much effort into other subjects as he did into using his computer.

'Morning, Rob,' said Elaine, looking up. 'Feeling bright today, are you?'

'All the brighter for seeing you, Elaine,' Rob said with a thin smile. 'Is that a new dress you've got on?'

'Yes, it is. Do you like it?'

Rob shook his head. 'Not really. But so long as you do, that's all that matters.'

Elaine Kirk tried not to show she was irritated, but Rob could tell from the way her mouth tightened that she was. *Good,* he thought. *Have a taste of your own medicine!*

For a reason that he couldn't quite explain, Rob had been feeling increasingly uncomfortable with Elaine Kirk. Over the past few weeks it seemed to him that she'd been getting – well, *nosier* was the only way he could describe it.

It started again as soon as she settled herself by his side. 'Have you been playing on your computer this morning?'

'I don't *play* on my computer,' Rob replied. 'I use it.'

'Oh, Rob. You'll be telling me next you haven't got any games on it.'

Rob said nothing.

'With your parents in the business and all? I bet you've got stacks of *GAMEZONE* programs on there, haven't you?'

'No, I haven't, as a matter of fact.'

'Really? You mean your dad doesn't bring home new ones for you to try out?'

'Why don't you ask him?' said Rob, annoyed.

It was Elaine Kirk's turn not to answer. With a forced smile, she ignored Rob's comment and pulled a book from the pile on the table.

'Simultaneous equations,' she said. 'I think we should spend the morning on those . . .'

Thursday 23 October, 12.05 p.m.

It was with a sigh of relief that, three hours later, Rob took his lunch to his room and left Elaine Kirk to eat hers on her own. Immediately, he turned on his computer. He wanted to check his e-mail.

Over the past months Rob had made some good contacts. Three, in particular, he exchanged notes with regularly. As his system came up, he quickly skimmed through the list of e-mail that had come in since his last session. There were four items waiting for him. He decided, with a smile, that one of them he would definitely leave until last!

Starting on the remaining three, he opened Tom's note first.

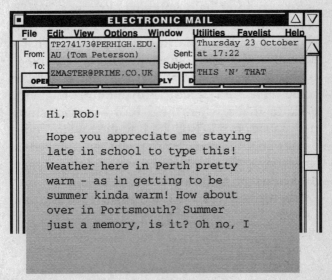

```
                    ELECTRONIC MAIL
  File    Edit  View  Options  Window  Utilities  Favelist  Help
          TP274173@PERHIGH.EDU.          Thursday 23 October
  From:   AU (Tom Peterson)        Sent: at 17:22
  To:                              Subject:
          ZMASTER@PRIME.CO.UK               THIS 'N' THAT
  OPE                             PLY  D


      Hi, Rob!

      Hope you appreciate me staying
      late in school to type this!
      Weather here in Perth pretty
      warm - as in getting to be
      summer kinda warm! How about
      over in Portsmouth? Summer
      just a memory, is it? Oh no, I
```

forgot. You don't have summer in
England!
Hey, guess what. I'm on the trail
of another one of us - y'know,
another Peterson. Picked him up by
chance on a chess bulletin board,
would you believe? Maybe he knows
about Prisoner 274183, huh?

Tom

Mail:

Rob couldn't help laughing. Prisoner 274183
was Tom Peterson's ancestor, or so he believed,
banished to Australia in a convict ship. That's
how come Rob had contacted him. Tom had post-
ed a note to a bulletin board asking if anyone
could tell him about Portsmouth, England,
because that's where he'd heard convict ships
had sailed from. Rob had replied with some
details about the city. Since then they'd stayed in
touch, swapping hints and tips about things they
discovered on the Internet.

He opened his next message. It was from
Lauren.

File Edit View Options Window Utilities Favelist Help

From: LKTORO@CTX.CO.CA

To: ZMASTER@PRIME.CO.UK

Sent Thursday 23 October at 06:58

Subject Nothing much

OPE   PLY

Morning Rob! (Tho' it's *real*
morning here)

Thanks for your note. No time to
reply now, 'cos Allie is nagging
on about my homework and the
state of my room as if it's real
important. The homework is
simps, stuff for dummies, and I
like my room the way it is.

I think she just wants me out of
the way so's she can log on
herself. She's got her own ID and
all. I ask you - 68 years old and
the woman's started surfing!

Lauren

Lauren King lived in Toronto, Canada, with
her grandmother, Alice. Rob laughed at the
thought of a grey-haired old lady throwing her
knitting in the bin and settling down for a few
hours on the Internet.

Two notes left to look at. He brought up the
one from New York; from his namesake, Mitch
Zanelli.

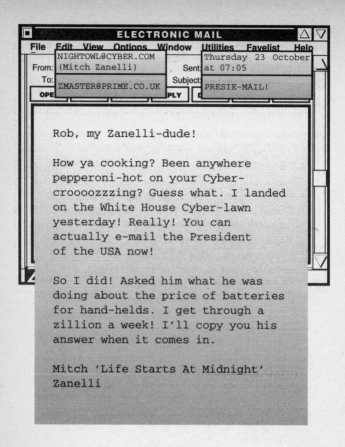

File   Edit   View   Options   Window   Utilities   Favelist   Help

From: NIGHTOWL@CYBER.COM
      (Mitch Zanelli)

To: ZMASTER@PRIME.CO.UK

Sent: Thursday 23 October
      at 07:05

Subject: PRESIE-MAIL!

OPE   PLY

Rob, my Zanelli-dude!

How ya cooking? Been anywhere
pepperoni-hot on your Cyber-
crooooozzzing? Guess what. I landed
on the White House Cyber-lawn
yesterday! Really! You can
actually e-mail the President
of the USA now!

So I did! Asked him what he was
doing about the price of batteries
for hand-helds. I get through a
zillion a week! I'll copy you his
answer when it comes in.

Mitch 'Life Starts At Midnight'
Zanelli

Total loon! thought Rob. Not like him at all, even though they shared the same surname. That was why Rob had contacted him in the first place, wondering if they were related. Since then, Rob had discovered that Mitch lived in New York, and worked as a washer-up in a café. It was a special type of café, though, with Internet computers for the customers to use without having to buy their own. By getting in extra-early, or staying extra-late, Mitch was allowed to log on for free.

Leaving his final note unread, Rob finished his lunch then loaded a file he'd discovered on the Internet about how to get news about space-shuttle launches from NASA in Florida. To save time, he turned the file into an e-mail note. At the end, he added

    :CC. ALL

ALL was the name of a mailing list he'd set up so that he could automatically send a copy of any note to Lauren, Tom and Mitch without having to type their full details every time.

With a quick click on the SEND button he sent the three copies of the note on their way.

Finally, he clicked on OPEN to read his fourth note, the one he'd deliberately saved until last. As he read it, his eyebrows rose. Here was a seriously annoyed person!

'Time to get started again, Rob.'

It was Elaine Kirk, her head round the door. Rob nodded. 'OK. Won't be a minute.'

Rob turned back to the screen and read the note again. This was starting to become fun! What could he say this time? He thought for a moment, then began typing.

He'd almost finished when Elaine Kirk stuck her head round the door once more. 'Ready?' she said.

'OK, OK. I'm nearly done.'

This time, though, Elaine Kirk didn't leave. Instead she slipped inside the door and stood, watching.

Rob could almost feel her eyes on him. With his mind not fully on what he was doing, Rob quickly finished his note, adding automatically:

```
:CC. ALL
```

before clicking on SEND.

'Finished. OK?' said Rob.

'No hurry,' said Elaine Kirk, casually moving closer to him.

Rob bridled. Was it his imagination, or was she trying to see what was on the screen, trying to see what he was up to? It was none of her business. Rob quickly set the shut-down procedure into motion and the screen was cleared.

He looked up in time to catch the look of annoyance in Elaine Kirk's eyes. *Good*, thought Rob. She couldn't have had time to take in any of it.

Not even the signature at the bottom of his note: ZMASTER!

Abbey School. 1.05 p.m.
Josh finished his lunch unhurriedly. He had agreed to meet Tamsyn in the Technology Block at one o'clock and it was already five past. No

problem. She probably wouldn't be there yet. Still in the school library with her head stuck in a book, more like. He smiled to himself as he remembered his downloading of *David Copperfield*. Good, that.

Ambling across the playground, Josh paused to watch a football match that was in progress. He enjoyed football – outdoors and indoors. As he watched he reminded himself that he hadn't got around to selling his World Cup game. Now that he knew he could win the trophy every time, it had become dead boring. Maybe there was a better version lurking somewhere on the Internet? He could have a surf around while he waited for Tamsyn.

Decision made, Josh picked up speed and pushed through the doors of the Technology Block. To his surprise, he found that Tamsyn was already at the computer and looking as though she wanted to play football herself – with the screen!

'Don't tell me you're getting hooked, Tamsyn?'

'Hooked?' spluttered Tamsyn. 'I tell you who should be hooked! This ZMASTER nut!'

'Huh?' said Josh.

Tamsyn explained to him about the e-mail she'd received the previous evening, then about her reply. When, finally, she showed him the note she'd found moments earlier, he couldn't help laughing.

'I think he's taken a shine to you,' laughed Josh as he read the note Rob had hurriedly fired off.

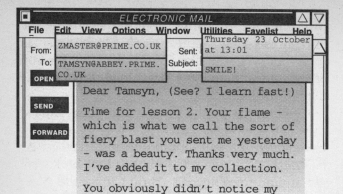

File   Edit   View   Options   Window   Utilities   Favelist   Help

From: ZMASTER@PRIME.CO.UK   Sent: Thursday 23 October at 13:01
To: TAMSYN@ABBEY.PRIME.CO.UK Subject: SMILE!

OPEN

SEND

FORWARD

Dear Tamsyn, (See? I learn fast!)

Time for lesson 2. Your flame –
which is what we call the sort of
fiery blast you sent me yesterday
– was a beauty. Thanks very much.
I've added it to my collection.

You obviously didn't notice my
smiley ...

'Huh?' said Tamsyn. 'What's he on about?'
'Read the next bit,' grinned Josh.

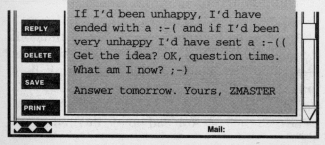

Come again? I can hear you
thinking. What's he on about?

What I'm on about is the :-) I
put after my name. Remember it?
It's the way e-mailers show each
other how they're feeling, 'cos
it's hard to do that in a note.
Turn your head sideways, so's
it's resting on your left
shoulder. See? A :-) looks like
a smiley face, and that's what I
sent you BECAUSE I WAS JOKING!

REPLY

DELETE

SAVE

PRINT

If I'd been unhappy, I'd have
ended with a :-(and if I'd been
very unhappy I'd have sent a :-((
Get the idea? OK, question time.
What am I now? ;-)

Answer tomorrow. Yours, ZMASTER

Mail:

'What are you?' muttered Tamsyn. 'I'll tell you—'

'Ah-ah,' broke in Josh. 'Gentleman present.' He looked more closely at the screen. 'Now *that's* interesting.'

'What is?'

'Scroll on a bit more.'

Tamsyn hit the down-arrow key on the keyboard, revealing that there was more to it than they'd actually been able to see.

'What does it mean?'

'I think it means he's just made a little bit of a mistake.'

```
Copied to:
TP274173@PERHIGH.EDU.AU (Tom Peterson)
LKTORO@CTX.CO.CA (Lauren King)
NIGHTOWL@CYBER.COM (Mitch Zanelli)
```

'It looks like he's copied his note to these others. Maybe they're all having a laugh about it. But he's forgotten to turn off the copy list. That's why it's tagged on the end like it is.'

Tamsyn stared at the screen. 'Hey – does that AU at the end of the "Tom" line mean Australia? Like – *the* Australia?'

Josh nodded. 'Must do. And this Lauren's in Canada – that's the CA – and Mitch is just COM, which means he's in America.'

'ZMASTER certainly gets about, doesn't he?' said Tamsyn before picking up on what Josh had said earlier. 'But why do you think showing us that list is a mistake?'

'Because, dummy,' said Josh, tapping the side of his nose, 'it gives you a way of getting your own back on him.'

'How?'

'By sending some notes to these Tom, Lauren and Mitch kids – whoever they are – making out they're from ZMASTER.'

'Saying what? I've just won the lottery and I'm going to split it with them?'

'Yeah,' grinned Josh. 'Something like that. Or . . . Hey, I know!'

Josh settled himself at the keyboard, his whole body moving energetically from side to side as he typed.

```
Dear Lauren,
Hi! Could you do me a favour?
For some reason I'm having
trouble downloading 'David
Copperfield' from the classic
books library. Could you do it
and FTX it to me? Thanks a lot.
ZMASTER
```

He finished with a flourish. 'What do you reckon?'

Tamsyn shrugged. 'So? What will that do?'

'What will it do?' said Josh. 'Do you know how long *David Copperfield* is?'

'Of course I do,' retorted Tamsyn. 'I've just read it, remember. It's over eight hundred pages.'

'Which means,' said Josh, emphasizing every word, 'it will really bung up ZMASTER's hard disk! And *three* copies will really really really bung it up! What do you reckon?'

As the idea sank in, Tamsyn's eyes lit up. Leaning across, she slid the keyboard away from Josh and towards her.

'I reckon you shouldn't have all the fun! Come on, let me type the others!'

CHAPTER 4

Manor House. Friday 24th October, 8.40 a.m.

The catches on Mr Zanelli's briefcase opened with a snap. Rob guessed what was coming from the smile on his father's face.

'Good news day,' said Mr Zanelli.

'We cut the gold diskette yesterday,' said Mrs Zanelli, coming into Rob's room to join them.

'So, superstition time,' said Mr Zanelli.

He pulled out an ordinary-looking black diskette, although Rob knew it was anything but ordinary.

'Bring us luck,' said Mrs Zanelli. 'Give it a try, as usual.'

'Just don't find any bugs in it,' said Mr Zanelli. 'That's something we can do without. We're on a tight enough schedule with this one as it is.'

Rob took the diskette from his father. *Lure of the Labyrinth* read the handwritten label. It was the latest computer game from *GAMEZONE*, one that Rob knew his parents' company had been working on for months.

This was the final test. It had become, as Mr Zanelli had said, a bit of a superstition.

They would develop a new game, testing it until they were as sure as they could be that it was perfect. Then they would cut what they called 'the gold diskette' – a single diskette with the finished version of the program on it. This they would bring home for Rob to try out for a week. If he couldn't break it, then they figured no other kid could.

The first time this had happened, over three years previously, Mr Zanelli had done it for a joke. Rob had immediately found a mistake in the program which, if the game had gone into the shops, would have cost *GAMEZONE* thousands of pounds to put right.

Mr Zanelli handed Rob the diskette. 'Guard it with your life,' he said, only half-joking.

'Of course,' said Rob. He tossed it casually onto his bed.

'Rob!'

'I know, I know,' said Rob.

He didn't have to be told how valuable that little diskette actually was. Every computer games company in the business would be prepared to pay good money to know what was on it. Keeping their games secret was a constant problem. Not so long ago one of *GAMEZONE*'s staff had been caught trying to hack into the development computer, presumably so that he could copy what was there and try to sell it.

The harsh buzz from the front door interrupted them. 'That will be Elaine now,' said Mrs Zanelli.

She bent to kiss Rob goodbye. 'Bye for now. See you this evening.'

Mr Zanelli followed her out. He paused at the door. 'You won't leave that there, will you?' he said, nodding towards the diskette on Rob's bed.

Rob laughed. 'Stay cool, Dad! I'll be trying it just as soon as Elaine lets me take a break.'

As Mr Zanelli left, Rob gathered his books together. He heard his parents talking to Elaine Kirk for a few moments, the dull babble of their voices coming up to him from the hallway. Then he heard the front door close.

Rob picked up the diskette from his bed and looked at it. *Lure of the Labyrinth*. Sounds good, he thought. It would be something to look forward to, a welcome relief from lessons.

Closing his door behind him, he headed off down the hallway and into the lounge.

10.15 a.m.

The chance came earlier than he expected. After an hour of English Literature, arguing about the character of Shylock in Shakespeare's *Merchant of Venice*, the front door bell rang sharply. Rob glanced towards the security panel mounted on the lounge wall – there was one in every room.

Elaine Kirk stopped twisting one of the expensive gold rings on her fingers, something Rob had noticed she'd been doing all morning, and got to her feet at once. 'I'll just see who it is,' she said, leaving the lounge quickly and closing the door behind her.

Rob was surprised. It was one of Mr Zanelli's strictest rules that, when he wasn't at home, the security speaker should always be used.

Elaine Kirk was soon back again. 'Charity collector,' she smiled. 'I gave him a pound and he went away happy.'

So why hadn't he heard voices?

Rob pushed the question to the back of his mind as Elaine said, 'Why don't you take some free time, Rob? Let's start again at . . .' she glanced at her watch, '. . . eleven. All right?'

'Sure,' said Rob, surprised again. They normally took a break about this time, but it was for fifteen minutes at the most then it was back to work.

Elaine Kirk opened the lounge door for him. 'Why don't you . . . I don't know, go and log in for a while? Yes, that's a good idea. I'll give you a shout when I'm ready.'

Rob headed slowly back down the hallway to his room, wondering what had made his tutor feel so generous. Whatever – free time was free time, and he wasn't going to argue.

Five minutes later he was logged in to the Internet and scanning his mail log. There was a message from Lauren – and, for some unaccountable reason, two very large files from Mitch and Tom.

He read Lauren's note first – and it explained everything.

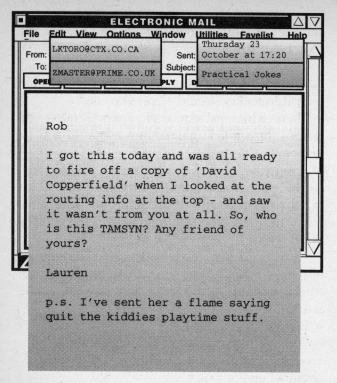

ELECTRONIC MAIL

File   Edit   View   Options   Window   Utilities   Favelist   Help

From: LKTORO@CTX.CO.CA   Sent: Thursday 23
                                        October at 17:20
To: ZMASTER@PRIME.CO.UK   Subject: Practical Jokes

OPE   PLY   D

Rob

I got this today and was all ready
to fire off a copy of 'David
Copperfield' when I looked at the
routing info at the top – and saw
it wasn't from you at all. So, who
is this TAMSYN? Any friend of
yours?

Lauren

p.s. I've sent her a flame saying
quit the kiddies playtime stuff.

Beneath it, Lauren had forwarded the note Josh
and Tamsyn had sent to her.

'Oh, good try!' Rob said, laughing out loud.

With a couple of quick commands, Rob deleted
the files that Mitch and Tom had sent him. Copies
of *David Copperfield* he assumed, they having read
only the message and not the address it had come
from like Lauren.

'Good try, Tamsyn,' he said again. 'I think I'm
starting to like you.'

He hit the SEND button. As the screen came up

with its empty page, Rob sat back and thought. What should he say to Tamsyn this time?

It was then that he heard the faintest sounds of whispering coming from the hallway.

'Elaine?' he called out. 'Is that you?'

The whispering stopped at once. He heard his tutor's footsteps moving quickly towards his room.

'Did you call me, Rob?' said Elaine Kirk, putting her head round his door.

'I thought I heard you talking. Is there somebody else here?'

'Somebody else? No, of course there isn't.' Elaine Kirk gave a short laugh. 'You must be hearing things, Rob. You're sure that's not a talking computer you've got there?'

Rob looked up at her. Looking slightly harassed in spite of her trim new suit, she was twisting the ring on her finger again – just as she had been before the bell went.

At that instant, as he remembered what she'd said after answering the door, he realized she'd lied to him. 'I gave him a pound and he went away happy,' that's what she'd said. But how could she? She hadn't taken her handbag with her!

And why hadn't she used the security speaker ... unless she'd been *expecting* somebody!

Rob pushed forward. Elaine Kirk barred his way. 'Where are you going?'

'Just for a wander,' said Rob. 'I do live here, you know.'

The tutor stepped aside reluctantly. 'You don't believe me, do you?' she said, quite loudly.

Rob didn't answer. As he went out into the hallway, he was listening intently.

Elaine Kirk followed him. 'It must have been me. Talking to myself, I suppose. First sign of madness, eh? Look, why don't you show me what you were doing on the Internet? I'm really interested . . .'

'When I've had my wander,' said Rob, heading for the spacious front hall, its glossy floor smelling of polish. 'There's nothing wrong with my ears, Elaine.'

When he reached it, he stopped.

'There you are, what did I tell you?' said Elaine Kirk from behind him. 'There's nobody else here. You're imagining things.'

Imagination? thought Rob. Was it his imagination or had she been speaking more loudly than usual? Loud enough to be heard by somebody in one of the other rooms in the house?

'Rob, this is silly!' Elaine Kirk called as he began turning round slowly, listening hard.

That was when he heard it.

Rob had spent so much time in this house, he knew every squeak of every chair, every rattle of every doorknob. And he knew that what he'd just heard was the sound of his father's study door being closed. Quickly he turned towards it.

'No, you don't.'

In an instant, Elaine Kirk had stepped forward and grabbed him by the shoulders. Rob struggled free, but again his tutor caught hold of him.

'Let me go!' shouted Rob. Again he broke away, moving swiftly towards his father's study door.

It opened just before he reached it.

'OK, kid. That's far enough.'

A short, stocky man had stepped out from the door. He had a smile on his lips, but his grey eyes showed no sign of doing the same.

Rob felt a sudden spasm of terror. 'Who are you?' he shouted.

The man's smile stayed in place. 'Why, don't you recognize me? Tut-tut. And me your daddy's favourite, too.'

Staring up, Rob searched the man's face for clues. He looked like he was in his mid-twenties. Above the grey eyes, his hair was parted in the centre and slicked back with gel. That was when Rob realized.

He'd seen this man at *GAMEZONE*, about six months ago, when he'd gone in to see the new development computer they'd just bought. The man now standing in Mr Zanelli's study doorway had been one of those who'd helped show him round.

'Brett Hicks,' Rob said quietly.

'Well done. Got it in one.'

'You work for my parents.'

'Worked,' said Hicks, his smile fading. 'Past tense. Your old man sacked me three months ago.'

'Sacked?' echoed Rob. Now he understood.

'You were the one caught trying to hack into the development computer, weren't you?'

Hicks nodded. 'Before I'd managed it. The thing was too well protected. But as it happened I'd have been too early. What I was after wasn't ready. Now it is . . .'

Rob looked at him. 'What do you mean?'

'Lure of the Labyrinth,' he said. 'My contacts tell me they cut the gold diskette yesterday.' Hicks's smile was back. 'And everybody in *GAMEZONE* knows that the big boss has a superstition. He always takes the diskette home with him for a few days to try it out.'

He looked behind him, into Mr Zanelli's study. 'So that's why I'm here, Rob. You don't mind me calling you Rob? You see, Rob, before your folks get back home I'm going to find that diskette – and take it.'

'W-why?' stammered Rob, although he knew the reason already.

'Come on, Rob. Elaine says you're smart. You know what that disk's worth. I can have a hundred thousand pirate copies of that game on the black market instantly. A hundred thousand copies at five pounds a time.'

'A cool half million pounds,' said Elaine Kirk. 'With both of us out of the country and out of reach.'

As his tutor spoke for the first time since Hicks had shown himself, Rob swung round. 'You – you're in with him, aren't you?' he said simply. 'Why?'

She shrugged. 'Money. As simple as that . . .'

Rob looked again at her smart new outfit, thought of all the other new clothes and jewellery she'd turned up wearing ever since she'd started tutoring him.

'. . . I love spending money.'

'I'd been looking for a way of getting back at your old man ever since he fired me,' said Brett Hicks. 'So when I met Elaine a few weeks ago . . . well, it all kind of slipped into place. It was just a matter of waiting for the right moment.'

He came round beside Rob and knelt down.

'And this is the moment.' Hicks's voice was cool and calm. 'I'm going to turn this place over until I find that disk.' He stood up again, and now his voice was harsher. 'Take him away somewhere, Elaine.'

'Where?'

'Anywhere. Who cares?' Hicks looked down at Rob. 'I mean, he's hardly likely to run for help, is he?'

He gave a sharp laugh as Elaine Kirk took Rob by the shoulders and spun him round. 'Good one, eh? Run for help!' Still smirking, Hicks turned back into Mr Zanelli's study.

Rob didn't bother to struggle. What could he do? Nothing. Hot tears stung his eyes as Elaine Kirk pushed him quickly back towards his room. Opening the door, she shoved him inside. The key turned in the lock of the solid door.

He's hardly likely to run for help, is he . . .

Hicks's cruel words echoed in Rob's mind. Of course he couldn't run for help. He hadn't been able to run since he was eight . . . since the accident.

In his anger and frustration, Rob slammed both hands down on the arms of his wheelchair. How often had he wished that he *could* run! How often had he wished he wasn't stuck in this room with just his computer for company.

His computer . . .

Rob looked at the blank e-mail page, still waiting patiently for him to type his message to Tamsyn.

That was it! He might not be able to run for help – but then perhaps he didn't need to. Perhaps he could call for help another way.

Quickly, he flicked on the CAPS LOCK key and began to type . . .

TAMSYN, GET HELP

But no sooner had he started than he heard Brett Hicks shouting outside, 'Elaine, has the kid got a computer? With e-mail on it?'

'Yes!'

'Then get it off! I don't want him sending messages . . .'

Rob didn't catch the rest. All he heard were Elaine Kirk's high heels as she started clattering back towards his room.

Rob's mind was in a whirl. What was he going to do? He didn't have time to spell out what had happened. The most he could do was . . . yes, it could work. If Tamsyn was smart.

Rob's fingers hammered repeatedly at the RETURN key until the three words he'd typed scrolled off the screen. Then, as he heard the scrape of the key turning in his door lock, he frantically typed some more characters.

Desperately, he flicked the mouse onto the SEND button and clicked once.

He was just in time.

No sooner had the door crashed open than Elaine Kirk was diving across the room to yank the modem cable from the telephone socket on the wall.

Back she came, her eyes scanning the screen, and the characters he'd just typed. Rob's heart was thumping. Would she understand what they meant?

'No problem!' shouted Elaine Kirk over her shoulder, as she turned off the computer.

Rob breathed a sigh of relief. She hadn't understood what he'd typed.

Brett Hicks came in. He stopped, looking at Rob's computer. 'Has he got games on there?'

Elaine Kirk shook her head. 'He says he hasn't. I asked him earlier.'

Hicks looked thoughtful. For a moment Rob thought he was going to turn the computer back on. Instead, he grabbed roughly at the handles of Rob's wheelchair and turned him round.

'I'm going to move you well away from that computer,' Hicks muttered.

As he was pushed roughly back into the lounge, Rob had never felt so alone.

Would his note do the trick? It was a long shot.

Elaine Kirk hadn't realized it was a call for help. So . . . would Tamsyn?

CHAPTER 5

Abbey School. 11.00 a.m.

'What on earth does it mean?' said Tamsyn. She was already beginning to regret letting Josh persuade her to miss morning break to check their e-mail.

'It means he's barmy,' said Josh. 'Out of his skull. Loopy. Read me?'

'I read you,' replied Tamsyn. 'What I can't read is that!'

Again, she and Josh stared at the e-mail on the screen.

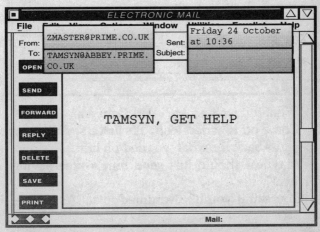

'Today's date,' said Tamsyn. 'So it can't be an April Fool's joke.'

Josh snorted. 'Maybe he does it all year round.'

Tamsyn shook her head slowly. Perhaps Josh was right, and it was just a stupid message to keep them guessing for a while. But if it was, why hadn't he said something about their *David Copperfield* trick – which hadn't worked very well, if the note from ZMASTER's friend Lauren was anything to go by:

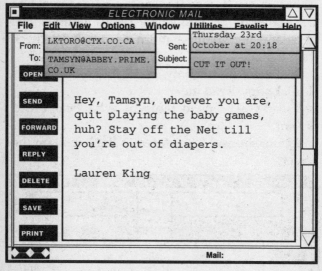

'What if it isn't a joke?' said Tamsyn.

'Come off it!' cried Josh. 'It's just a sad attempt to get us back for what we tried on him.'

'Maybe I should just send him a note saying "Truce!"'

'You can if you like,' grunted Josh. 'As for me,

I'd pull the plug on friend ZMASTER. I've got better things to do with my time. Like getting started on this report we're supposed to be writing for Mr Findlay, remember?' He got to his feet, as if to go.

Tamsyn nodded. 'I haven't forgotten, Josh.' She tapped a finger against the computer screen. 'So why can't we use this in our report? If the Internet can be used just to play silly jokes . . .'

'Which it can,' grinned Josh, 'because we tried it!'

'Well, shouldn't we say so in our report?' She looked again at the message from ZMASTER. 'If this *is* a silly joke, that is.'

Sighing, Josh came back and sat down beside her again. Out loud, he read, 'TAMSYN, GET HELP'.

'In capitals,' added Tamsyn. 'In an e-mail, he said that was like shouting.'

'So?'

'So why is ZMASTER doing it himself?

Josh shrugged. 'Search me. Is there any more?'

After the little bit they could see, there was just the large blank space caused by Rob's repeated pressing of the RETURN key to scroll his message off the screen before Elaine Kirk saw it.

Tamsyn hit the PAGE DOWN key on the keyboard.

'The plot thickens,' whistled Josh. 'Now tell me he's not playing games.'

The tail end of the message, the last part that Rob had so hurriedly typed and which had made no sense at all to Elaine Kirk, was there in front of them.

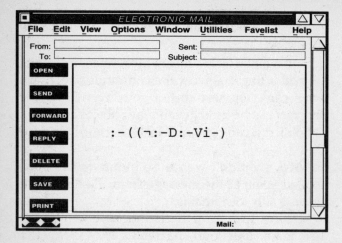

'What does that lot mean?' said Tamsyn.

'Looks like a string of smileys to me,' said Josh. 'Remember his previous note?'

Tamsyn did. Quickly – and with a speed that surprised her – she clicked on the MAIL LOG icon and retrieved the previous note they'd had from ZMASTER. This time she read it coolly, rather than in a boiling rage ...

```
What I'm on about is the :-) I
put after my name. Remember it?
It's the way e-mailers show each
other how they're feeling, 'cos
it's hard to do that in a note.
Turn your head sideways, so's
it's resting on your left
shoulder. See? A :-) looks like
```

```
a smiley face, and that's what I
sent you BECAUSE I WAS JOKING!

If I'd been unhappy, I'd have
ended with a :-(
```

It was the next part of the note that suddenly made Tamsyn sit up with a jolt . . .

```
and if I'd been very unhappy I'd
have sent a :-((
```

Again she brought up the message they'd just received. If she ignored the big blank space in the middle, it came to

```
TAMSYN, GET HELP :-((¬:-D:-Vi-)
```

'Look,' she said. 'Those first four characters. Colon, dash, left bracket, left bracket. Meaning he's very unhappy.'

Josh cackled. 'Maybe our *David Copperfield* trick did work then! Maybe his hard disk is totally bunged up and he is very unhappy!'

As the bell went to signal the end of morning break, Tamsyn quickly copied down the row of peculiar characters. She was intrigued. What was ZMASTER up to? Was this a sort of super-smiley he'd sent, or was it more? A coded message of some sort?

So, Josh was probably right. ZMASTER probably was just playing a game and, if the string of characters turned out to say anything at all, it would be something incredibly stupid. But even if that proved to be the case, the fact that she'd been smart enough to crack the code would bug ZMASTER something wicked . . .

Logging off quickly, Tamsyn snatched up her bag and dashed off to catch up with Josh.

Manor House. 11.15 a.m.

In the lounge, Rob sat and waited. Opposite him, almost as if they were having a normal tutorial session, sat a silent Elaine Kirk.

'You can't get away with this,' said Rob.

Elaine Kirk smiled. 'No? Let's see.'

She looked up as Brett Hicks opened the door noisily and came in. 'Any luck?'

Hicks shook his head angrily. 'Nothing. I've been through every drawer and filing cabinet. And I haven't found any safe in there. I thought you said there was one.'

Elaine Kirk looked confused. 'Well . . . I'm sure I heard Mr Zanelli mention one once. But . . .' she looked at Hicks uncertainly, 'I haven't ever *seen* it, Brett. I've looked a few times. Maybe it's one of those hidden ones.'

Hicks took a step towards Rob. 'And maybe this young man knows exactly *where* it's hidden, eh?'

'I don't!' shouted Rob at once.

'I don't know if I believe you, Rob,' said Hicks quietly. 'I reckon you could be lying. Are you?'

Rob simply glared at him in defiance.

Hicks's cool manner broke suddenly. Snatching at the front of Rob's jumper, he pulled him forward. 'Are you?' he shouted.

'Brett!' Elaine Kirk looked shocked.

Hicks immediately let go. Rob sank back into his wheelchair. Hicks stood up, calm again. He turned away and went back to the door.

'I'm going to look for that safe. If I find it, good. If not . . .' He looked at Elaine Kirk, nervously twisting her rings, then down at Rob. '. . . I'll be talking to you again.'

The chill in his voice made Rob's stomach tighten. How long had he got? Hicks knew about Mr Zanelli's practice of bringing home gold diskettes. What he obviously didn't know was that it was Rob who tried them out.

He had to say or do what he could to keep Hicks searching for the *Lure of the Labyrinth* diskette in his father's study and away from his own room. He had to keep him off the trail for as long as he could . . . had to give this Tamsyn girl enough time to work out what he'd tried to tell her.

If she *could* work it out . . .

Abbey School. 11.40 a.m.
'Tamsyn Smith, are you here today?'

Tamsyn looked up. At the front of the class Ms Gillies, her English teacher, was not looking best pleased.

'Sorry, Ms Gillies?'

'I asked you to explain what I mean by "parsing a sentence".'

'Er . . . parsing?'

'A sentence,' repeated Ms Gillies. She waited expectantly, her horn-rimmed spectacles glinting in the classroom's strip lights.

Tamsyn tried to get her mind in focus. She'd tried to concentrate on the lesson, but found her mind coming back time and time again to ZMASTER's curious message. Even as she tried to answer Ms Gillies' question her eyes were straying towards the odd series of characters she'd scribbled down on the cover of her notebook.

'Parsing a sentence,' said Tamsyn slowly. 'That's . . . er . . . splitting a sentence into its different parts . . .'

'Close,' said Ms Gillies icily. 'Try this sentence: "The teacher waited patiently." '

Tamsyn gulped. 'Er . . . "Teacher" is the subject noun. "Waited" is the verb. "Patiently" is an adverb . . .'

'And "The"?'

'Er . . . definite article?'

The English teacher nodded slowly, surprised that Tamsyn could have come up with such a decent answer when it was clear she hadn't been listening to a word she'd been saying. She looked around, hoping for more success by picking on somebody else.

As Ms Gillies' gimlet eye left her, Tamsyn

returned to studying the string of characters.

'Parsing!' she breathed to herself as soon as she looked down.

It was obvious. This wasn't one big super-smiley, but a number of them joined together – a *collection* of smileys. What she had to do was divide them up!

```
:-((¬:-D:-Vi-)
```

But how did they divide up? Surely, the first had to be

```
:-((
```

– the one which looked like a really sad face. ZMASTER would be aware that she knew that one. He'd mentioned it in the e-mail she'd gone through with Josh. Tamsyn thought about it. Perhaps the start of ZMASTER's message was:

TAMSYN, GET HELP. I'M VERY UNHAPPY.

If so, what about the rest of the line? How did it divide up into different smileys? Making sure that Ms Gillies wasn't looking her way, Tamsyn turned her head to one side. After some seconds peering at them, Tamsyn picked up her pencil and doodled a rough separation for the rest of the line.

```
¬:-D    :-V    i-)
```

Three separate smileys? And, if so, what did each of them mean?

As the bell went for the end of the lesson Ms Gillies swept from the room, pausing only to cast a withering look in Tamsyn's direction.

Josh came straight over. 'She had her eye on you all period,' he said. 'What on earth were you up to?'

Quickly Tamsyn spread out her doodling on the desk. 'I was trying to crack this. It's a message, I'm sure it is. "Tamsyn, get help. I'm very unhappy . . ." I just can't see what the rest means.'

Josh shook his head at once. 'It means,' he said, 'have some lunch. He's having us on.'

'How can you say that?' said Tamsyn. Josh sounded so certain.

'Look at that one,' said Josh, tapping the second group in the row on Tamsyn's notebook.

¬ : −D

'What does that remind you of?' said Josh.

Turning her head to one side, Tamsyn saw it at once. Cursing herself for being so stupid as to think, even for an instant, that it might be a serious message, she muttered, 'Somebody with a funny hat on – and a laughing face.'

Josh nodded. 'In other words, "I'm joking." Right?'

'Right,' sighed Tamsyn. 'A joke.'

Gathering her books together, Tamsyn wandered idly out of the classroom, leaving Josh to go on ahead. Outside, the weather was looking good. She would forget all about computers and electronic mail and smileys for the next hour and find a nice quiet non-electronic tree to sit under.

'Tamsyn! How's the Internet project getting along?' asked Mr Findlay, hurrying her way.

'Fine,' said Tamsyn.

'You're getting into it? Not letting Josh run the show?'

Tamsyn fished in her bag and pulled out the first few pages of the report they'd prepared. 'Not likely. This is a joint effort.'

Looking pleased, the teacher took the report from her. He skimmed through the pages. He stopped only once, at the bottom of the final page, to pencil mark a comment in the margin.

Tamsyn looked at it – and gasped.

¬ B

'What does that mean?' she asked.

'Not bad,' said Mr Findlay. 'B for bad . . .'

Tamsyn was ahead of him. 'And that 'L' on its side means "Not"?' she said.

'Certainly does,' smiled the teacher. 'You're a little way off whizz-kid level yet then, Tamsyn, otherwise you'd know that. It's often called the NOT symbol. It's used in a lot of programming languages to mean, "take what comes next, and turn it round . . ." '

He didn't get a chance to finish. Tamsyn spun on her heel and with a shout of, 'Sorry, got to fly!' hared after Josh as fast as she could go.

She found him, sitting on a wall, munching a sandwich. 'Come on,' yelled Tamsyn pushing him in the back and off the wall. 'We've got work to do.'

'Huh?' mumbled Josh.

Tamsyn wrenched her notebook from her bag and pointed at the second part of the ZMASTER message.

'I got it wrong,' she yelled. 'That isn't a funny hat! Mr Findlay just told me. That symbol stands for "not".'

Josh just looked at her dumbly.

Tamsyn was almost jumping up and down. 'Don't you see? That part of the message doesn't mean "I'm joking". It means the exact opposite!'

She wrote it out on the cover of her notebook.

TAMSYN, GET HELP. VERY UNHAPPY.
NOT JOKING.

CHAPTER 6

Abbey School. 12.35 p.m.

This time it was Tamsyn who led the way to the Technology Block. Josh straggled in behind her, carrying half a sandwich and hiccuping madly.

'What exactly – *hic* – are you – *hic* – doing?' he said as he pulled up a chair and flopped down.

Tamsyn waited impatiently for the system to come up. 'If he *is* serious,' she said, 'if he *is* in some sort of trouble, then we've got to help him.'

Josh brushed the last crumbs from the front of his jumper. 'Even if – and there's a lot of ifs round here, Tamsyn – even if you are right, I don't see what we can do about it anyway. We don't know a thing about him.'

Tamsyn bit her lip. Josh was right. Apart from his User ID of ZMASTER, they knew nothing about the sender of the coded message – not his real name, not his real address . . . nothing.

'We could get hold of the company who run the Internet service, couldn't we? They must know who ZMASTER is.'

'Not without checking their records,' said Josh.

'Anyway, they wouldn't give out that information. It's confidential.'

In front of her, the computer screen flicked up its menu page. 'Then can't we use *something* on the system to find out?' she cried. 'Isn't that what computers are supposed to be for, to give you information?'

'Hey, how about that?' Josh was pointing at an item on the Internet start screen. It was marked WHOIS.

Tamsyn didn't think twice. She clicked on it.

```
      PRIME INTERNET SERVER:
          WHOIS FUNCTION
      Use this facility to discover
    details about any Internet user.

    Type in the User ID for which
           you require details:
```

'Brilliant!' she cried. Quickly she typed:

```
                 ZMASTER
```

The answer flicked up almost instantaneously:

```
No details available. User has not
  supplied personal information for
                WHOIS.
```

'What?' cried Tamsyn. 'That's rubbish! What's that supposed to mean?'

Josh was thumbing through the manual Mr Findlay had given them. 'Yes, here it is.' He read quickly through the text, before shaking his head. 'It says here that WHOIS uses the equivalent of a telephone directory. It only gives details supplied to it by users themselves.'

'And ZMASTER hasn't supplied anything?'

'Doesn't look like it.'

Tamsyn gave a frustrated sigh. Why weren't things simple? If she was right, and ZMASTER was in trouble, then she had to do something. And if the Internet couldn't help, what use was it at all?

Josh leaned across to bring up the e-mail system. He clicked on the SEND button. 'Fire him off a note. Ask what's going on.'

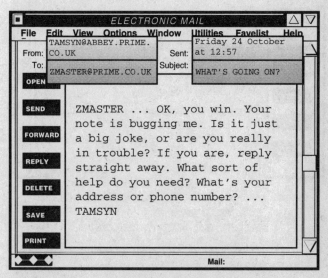

'Now what?' said Tamsyn, clicking on SEND again to fire the note on its way.

'That's it,' said Josh. 'That's all you can do.'

Tamsyn felt her blood beginning to boil. That *wasn't* all she could do. There had to be more. Yes! she realized. There *was* more. Quickly she brought up ZMASTER's coded note.

'What are you up to?' said Josh.

'I'm going to copy this to Lauren King, whoever she is. She's been in touch with ZMASTER for a while. Maybe she can tell us more about him.'

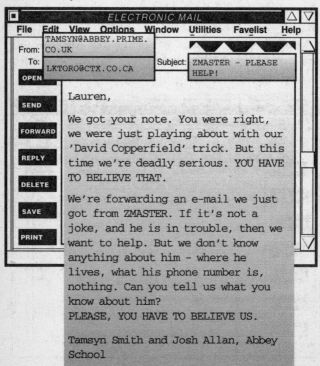

ELECTRONIC MAIL

File   Edit   View   Options   Window   Utilities   Favelist   Help

From: TAMSYN@ABBEY.PRIME.CO.UK

To: LKTORO@CTX.CO.CA   Subject: ZMASTER - PLEASE HELP!

OPEN
SEND
FORWARD
REPLY
DELETE
SAVE
PRINT

Lauren,

We got your note. You were right, we were just playing about with our 'David Copperfield' trick. But this time we're deadly serious. YOU HAVE TO BELIEVE THAT.

We're forwarding an e-mail we just got from ZMASTER. If it's not a joke, and he is in trouble, then we want to help. But we don't know anything about him - where he lives, what his phone number is, nothing. Can you tell us what you know about him?
PLEASE, YOU HAVE TO BELIEVE US.

Tamsyn Smith and Josh Allan, Abbey School

Tamsyn clicked on SEND. Would it work? Were they just being made fools of? She didn't know.

But as they went back for their afternoon classes, something inside her was saying that she just had to find out.

Manor House. 12.50 p.m.

'Bring him in here,' snapped Brett Hicks.

Rob didn't struggle this time; he just allowed Elaine Kirk to push his wheelchair across the hallway and right into Mr Zanelli's study.

'Over there,' said Hicks, motioning with a jabbing finger to a spot beside Mr Zanelli's carved oak desk.

Rob looked round. The place was a shambles. Hicks had turned out everything, looked everywhere. Each of the three filing cabinets had been forced open and the drawers emptied. The pictures that had been hanging on the walls were now in one corner, tossed into an untidy heap as Hicks had searched behind them for the safe.

Brett Hicks showed no emotion as he moved closer, but Rob could see the anger in his eyes. Rob was going to have to be careful, not push him too far.

Hicks bent down, his voice showing the strain of keeping his anger in check. 'The safe, Rob. Where is it?'

'I . . . I don't know,' he said.

'Don't know? Or won't tell?'

'I don't . . . remember,' Rob said finally.

Rob saw the look of satisfaction flicker across Hicks's face. 'Then try to remember. And make it quick!'

With a sudden thrust of his hand, Hicks grabbed Rob's shoulders and slammed him violently against the back of his chair.

'Brett, give over!' cried Elaine Kirk.

'Shut up!'

'Then leave him alone. Please! This was going to be easy, you said.'

Rob glanced up at his tutor's frightened face. Was she now seeing a side of Hicks that she hadn't seen before?

Hicks released his grip. 'Where's the safe?' he said slowly. To Rob it sounded as if every word was dripping with menace.

'Rob,' said Elaine Kirk, sounding scared herself now, 'if you know, tell him.'

Hicks was nodding, a smirk on his face. 'Listen to your tutor, Rob. She's giving you good advice—'

The shrill sound of the telephone interrupted him. Swinging round, Hicks stared at the red telephone on Mr Zanelli's desk as if it was a snake. As it continued to ring, he quickly clamped a hand over Rob's mouth.

'Answer it,' he snapped at Elaine Kirk.

Hesitantly, Rob's tutor picked up the receiver and held it to her ear. 'Hello? Zanelli residence.'

Rob wanted to shout, cry out, but Hicks's hand was holding him tight. All he could do was to make a low groaning sound from the pit of his stomach, not enough to be heard by whoever was calling.

It was his mother, Rob realized as Elaine Kirk spoke.

'Hello, Mrs Zanelli. Yes, everything's fine. Sorry? You'll probably be late?' Elaine Kirk flashed a glance their way. 'No, that's OK. I can stay on till you both get home. Not before six, you say? No problem, Mrs Zanelli. See you then. Bye.'

As the receiver was replaced and Hicks let him go, Rob slumped back in his wheelchair.

'That gives us another four or five hours, Rob,' said Hicks quietly. 'Just think what I could do to you and this place in four or five hours.'

He paused to let the threat sink in. 'So. The safe. Where is it?'

Now was the time, Rob decided.

He inched forward in his chair, scanning the ornate wood panelling of his father's study, with its intricate patterns of loops and whorls tumbling around large circular flowers. It was here somewhere, he knew it was. In those carefree days before his accident he'd been able to find it almost without looking.

Yes, that one, he thought. Stretching up, he ran his fingers over the carved woodwork towards one particular flower. He paused for just a moment – then pressed hard on the flower's centre.

Smoothly, a section of the panelling slid back. Behind it, a dial and a handle protruding from its flat square door, was a safe.

Brett Hicks's face creased into a smile. 'Well done.' He bent to look Rob in the eye. 'Very sensible.'

Behind him, Elaine Kirk sounded relieved. 'Come on, Brett. Get it open and let's get out of here.'

Hicks nodded. Swiftly he began unloading a small gas canister and a torch from a canvas bag, talking as he did so.

'You know what I've been doing since your old man sacked me, Rob? Me, a top computer programmer? Fixing cars. Welding rusty bodywork. Because after what happened, there's no way I can get another computer job. All thanks to your old man.'

Joining a small pipe to the end of the torch, Hicks turned a knob on the top of the canister. He struck a match and held it to the end of the torch. At once a crackling blue flame jetted out from the end of it.

'Funny, though. Welding cars has taught me one very useful skill.' He lifted the torch. 'You know what this is?'

'An oxyacetylene torch,' said Rob.

'Very good. You're right, Elaine. He is smart.'

Elaine Kirk gave him a weak smile.

'An oxyacetylene torch. As used for welding. But it can also cut through metal like butter.' Hicks turned towards the safe. 'Metal such as that door's made of. I don't know how thick it is, but I'll be through it soon enough. And knowing I've got some time to spare is a great help!'

He turned again to Elaine Kirk. 'Take him back, Elaine. I'll call you when I'm done.'

Rob felt himself being turned and pushed. He didn't know how long it would take Hicks to cut through the door of that safe. All he could hope was that it would keep him busy for long enough to allow Tamsyn to unscramble his message and get help.

If she *could* get help . . .

CHAPTER 7

Toronto, Canada.
7.45 a.m. (UK time 12.45 p.m.)
Lauren King loved the early Toronto mornings.
She would often get up and pad into the living
room of the small third-floor apartment she lived
in with her grandmother, Alice. There she would
stare out of the window, watching the traffic
build up in Yonge Street as workers set off for
their offices downtown.

And then her computer would beep, and she
would immediately turn away from the window
and get down to some serious work. Lauren King
was eleven years old, and she knew what she
liked.

Logging in to the Internet, Lauren quickly
scanned her mail log to see if there'd been any
reaction from Tamsyn-whoever to the message
she'd sent the day before. Nothing. Quitting her
e-mail package, Lauren began checking out one
of the dozen or so newsgroups she subscribed to.

'And what time do you call this, young lady?'
came a kindly voice from behind her shoulder.

Lauren turned and looked up at her plump

grandmother. Alice King had adopted her after Lauren's parents had drowned in a sailing accident.

'Nearly eight, Allie,' she said, using the only name she could ever remember calling her grandmother.

'You got time for that before school?' said Alice. 'Don't you think you should be logging off and getting ready?'

Lauren gave her grandmother a knowing look. 'So that you can log in yourself, Allie? You think I don't know what you get up to while I'm at school? I found two whole detective novels downloaded onto the hard disk the other day.'

Alice laughed. 'And why not? Just because I'm a lot older, it don't mean I can't go sailing the Net like you!'

'*Surfing* the Net, Allie. It's called surfing the Net.'

'Surfing, sailing – whatever. It's fun!' And with a call of, 'Another ten minutes, huh?' Alice headed off to the kitchen.

Lauren called after her, 'Anyway, you're out of luck today, Allie. School's closed, remember? Faculty training.'

Tamsyn's e-mail arrived seconds later, the warning beep sending Lauren straight into her mail package to open it.

She was still reading Tamsyn's message, and the ZMASTER note she'd forwarded, when Alice came back in carrying plates of waffles and maple syrup.

'Time's up,' called Alice. 'Come in, number eleven-year-old.' She sat down at their small table. 'You hear me, missie? Time's up.'

Still Lauren didn't move. 'What kind of fool game is this?' she muttered. Alice got up from the table and walked over to where Lauren was sitting. On the screen was Tamsyn's note, with that of ZMASTER beneath it.

'Smileys,' said Alice, seeing Rob's code line.

'I don't know who this Tamsyn girl is, but Rob's sent her a dumb message. She thinks it's for real.' Lauren sighed. 'I don't know. It's certainly *from* Rob to her – the routing information is right, this time.'

'Huh?'

'The stuff at the top, Allie. Telling you where the message has come from. Yesterday they tried to send me something pretending to be Rob and I spotted it.'

'Not that,' said Alice. 'I wasn't going "huh" at that. I was going "huh" at those smileys.' Putting on her glasses, she peered down at Rob's message on the screen.

```
:-((¬:-D:-Vi-)
```

'He's written GET HELP,' said Lauren. 'And they think the first two smileys mean "I'm very unhappy. I'm not joking." They don't know what the last two stand for. And neither do I.'

'Really? Well,' she chuckled, 'I can't duck a chance of working out something you can't!

Come on, let old Allie get a proper look.' She turned her head on one side. 'What does that V look like?'

```
: -V
```

'A funnel?' suggested Lauren. 'A cone?'

Alice wrinkled her nose. 'How about a megaphone!'

'What's a megaphone?'

'Something people used to shout through before microphones were invented.'

Lauren looked at the screen. 'So that smiley could mean "I'm shouting"?'

'Or calling,' said Alice. Her eyes narrowed. 'Maybe just "Call".'

'Call what? Whatever that last one stands for, I reckon.' She shook her head. 'That's a new one on me.'

```
i-)
```

'Me too,' said Alice. She turned her head to the side again. 'An "i" sounds like "eye". Maybe it's something to do with eyes. It looks like somebody with one eye closed. Hey – how about a fighter?'

'Call a fighter?' said Lauren. 'Come on, Allie. That wouldn't make sense. Rob's a smart guy.'

Alice stood up and looked in the living-room mirror. She closed one eye. 'OK,' she said. 'What does it look like I'm doing?'

'Looking through a telescope at something,' suggested Lauren. 'Or a microscope. Looking hard with that one eye, anyway.'

'It feels like I'm spying on somebody,' said Alice.

Lauren looked hard at her grandmother. 'Call a spy? No, that doesn't make sense either.'

'Not a spy!' said Alice, suddenly swinging round. 'An eye! A *private* eye! I bet that's what it stands for!'

Lauren looked at her grandmother. 'Private eye? You mean . . . a detective?'

'Policeman, in other words.'

Lauren stared at the screen. ' "Tamsyn, get help. Very unhappy. Not joking. Call police." Allie, do you really think it could mean that?'

'If there's the slightest chance it does, then we've got to do something.' Alice pulled a chair to the side of her granddaughter. 'Can you think of any way you can help this girl?'

Lauren pulled a box of diskettes from beside the computer and opened the lid. 'I can send her a file Rob sent me a while back. It contains a map of the area he lives in. It's on one of these diskettes.'

'One of those diskettes?' Alice had a frozen look on her face.

'Yes. Why, Allie?'

'Just that . . .' Alice gulped. 'Well . . . I've kinda been using them diskettes lately . . .'

Cyber-Snax Café, New York, USA.
8.10 a.m. (UK time 1.10 p.m.)

Mitch rubbed the sleep from his eyes and checked his watch. Ten past eight in the morning. It wasn't *human!* The things he'd do for a spin in cyberspace.

Letting himself into the café by the back door, Mitch flicked on a light. In the stockroom he could hear the manager already at work.

'Morning, Mr Lewin!'

'Morning, Mitch,' called a voice. 'Not too much surfing this morning, right? There's plenty for you to do.'

Heading on into the café, Mitch saw what Mr Lewin meant. Tables needed clearing, floors needed mopping – and for what? A pretty crummy wage . . . but also free net-surfing! It made it all worthwhile.

Mitch had spotted Cyber-Snax one day on his way home from jogging in Central Park. It was just being fitted out, a month before it opened. Inside twenty minutes Mitch had talked the owner into giving him a job.

So, it meant getting up every day at unearthly hours, when any sensible 17-year-old was still in bed. But this was a dream come true for Mitch. From his end of New York, the only way most kids got near a computer was by stealing one.

He logged in and found Lauren's note straight away.

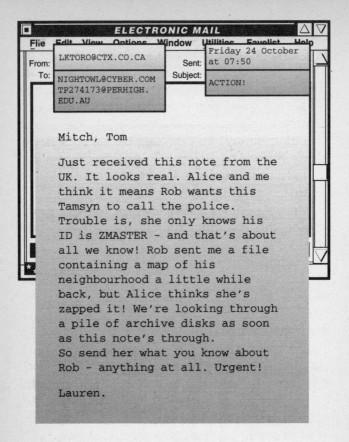

Flie   Edit   View   Options   Window   Utilities   Favelist   Help

From: LKTORO@CTX.CO.CA

To: NIGHTOWL@CYBER.COM
TP274173@PERHIGH.
EDU.AU

Sent: Friday 24 October
at 07:50

Subject: ACTION!

Mitch, Tom

Just received this note from the
UK. It looks real. Alice and me
think it means Rob wants this
Tamsyn to call the police.
Trouble is, she only knows his
ID is ZMASTER - and that's about
all we know! Rob sent me a file
containing a map of his
neighbourhood a little while
back, but Alice thinks she's
zapped it! We're looking through
a pile of archive disks as soon
as this note's through.
So send her what you know about
Rob - anything at all. Urgent!

Lauren.

Quickly, Mitch began to type . . .

Perth, Australia.
9.15 p.m. (UK time 1.15 p.m.)
'Tom! Are you ready, Tom!'

As his mother's voice echoed down the empty
school corridor, Tom Peterson looked at the clock

in the top corner of his screen. Nine fifteen. Bad news.

The voice went on. 'I'll be done in fifteen minutes! Don't make me wait around for you like yesterday. Your dad said he'd be home early tonight. So start finishing off now!'

Tom checked the clock again. There was no doubt about it. His mum was getting faster at her evening job cleaning at his school, East Perth High. He'd have to start thinking of ways to slow her down. Tom made a mental note to begin a 'make more mess for Mum during the day' campaign. His pals should be able to handle that for a small consideration.

The beep telling him that some mail had just arrived sounded loud in the quiet computer room. Tom hesitated. Should he chance looking at it now? He'd kept his mum waiting for nearly half an hour the night before and the meal she'd put in the oven for his dad's supper had been ruined. His dad, a detective with the Perth police, had blown a fuse when he'd got home to find a lump of charred chicken waiting for him on the table.

'All day staking out a robbery that doesn't happen,' he'd yelled, 'and I come home to this!'

Tom hesitated. Should he open this e-mail and risk keeping his mum waiting again? It would only take a minute or so.

Hunching forward, Tom clicked on the OPEN icon. Lauren's note, copied to himself and Mitch, flashed up onto the screen at once.

Tom stared at it for a minute, uncertain about what to do next. He hardly knew anything about Rob. Or did he?

What was it his dad always said? Any fact, however small, can make all the difference to an investigation.

The clatter of a bucket being shoved in a cupboard stirred him into action. Quickly, Tom began to type:

```
Tamsyn, all I know about
      ZMASTER is...
```

CHAPTER 8

Abbey School. 3.30 p.m.

Tamsyn could hardly wait until the end of school. Almost before the bell had finished ringing, she was haring out of her classroom and racing off towards the Technology Block again. Her enthusiasm was infectious. Even Josh began ambling a little faster as he saw her sprinting away.

She saw the status line reading MAIL: 2 ITEMS WAITING as soon as she logged in. Tamsyn's heart sank as she saw that neither of the notes were from Lauren King. They were from the other two IDs on ZMASTER's mailing list. Expecting more flames about the *David Copperfield* trick, Tamsyn opened them.

Moments later, she was staring at the screen in excitement. In the time she'd been in class that afternoon, messages had been flying around the globe!

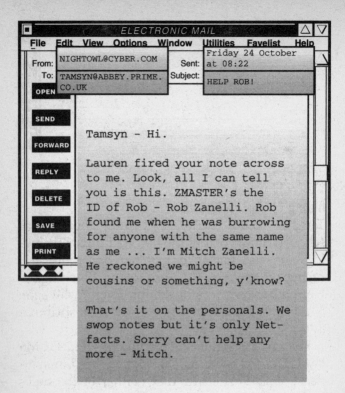

Tamsyn - Hi.

Lauren fired your note across
to me. Look, all I can tell
you is this. ZMASTER's the
ID of Rob - Rob Zanelli. Rob
found me when he was burrowing
for anyone with the same name
as me ... I'm Mitch Zanelli.
He reckoned we might be
cousins or something, y'know?

That's it on the personals. We
swop notes but it's only Net-
facts. Sorry can't help any
more - Mitch.

'Zanelli!' cried Tamsyn as Josh hurried through
the door. 'His name's Zanelli. Rob Zanelli.'

'Zanelli,' said Josh. 'That figures. Z for
ZMASTER.'

Tamsyn turned back to the screen and checked
the other e-mail. It was from Tom.

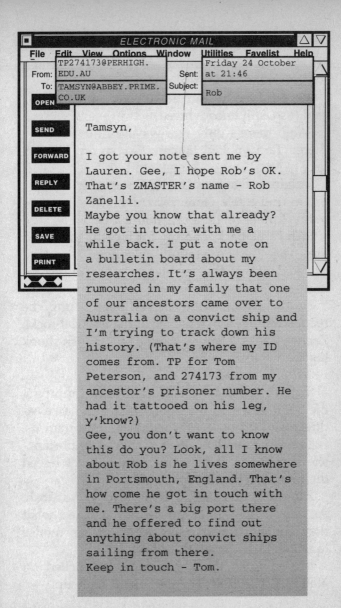

File Edit View Options Window Utilities Favelist Help

From: TP274173@PERHIGH.EDU.AU

To: TAMSYN@ABBEY.PRIME.CO.UK

Sent: Friday 24 October at 21:46

Subject: Rob

OPEN
SEND
FORWARD
REPLY
DELETE
SAVE
PRINT

Tamsyn,

I got your note sent me by
Lauren. Gee, I hope Rob's OK.
That's ZMASTER's name - Rob
Zanelli.
Maybe you know that already?
He got in touch with me a
while back. I put a note on
a bulletin board about my
researches. It's always been
rumoured in my family that one
of our ancestors came over to
Australia on a convict ship and
I'm trying to track down his
history. (That's where my ID
comes from. TP for Tom
Peterson, and 274173 from my
ancestor's prisoner number. He
had it tattooed on his leg,
y'know?)
Gee, you don't want to know
this do you? Look, all I know
about Rob is he lives somewhere
in Portsmouth, England. That's
how come he got in touch with
me. There's a big port there
and he offered to find out
anything about convict ships
sailing from there.
Keep in touch - Tom.

'And he lives in Portsmouth!' yelled Tamsyn. 'That's why he's asking *us* to get help – because we live in the same area!'

'Or because he can make right mugs of us,' said Josh, still unconvinced.

'Well, there's only one way to find out, isn't there!' Tamsyn said fiercely. 'So, go on! I'll wait here to see if Lauren King e-mails us.'

Josh looked at her. 'Go on? Go on what?'

'Go find a telephone directory. There can't be many Zanellis in the Portsmouth area!'

Josh came back, panting for breath. Under his arm was the Portsmouth telephone directory, sneaked out of the secretary's office under his jumper.

He flicked almost to the last page. 'Yung,' he read, scanning down the list of names. 'Zabrocki, Zacher, Zacks, Zambra, Zawodski . . .' Josh shook his head. 'No Zanelli.'

'What? Why not?'

'I don't know why not,' said Josh, thumping the book down on the floor. 'Because they're ex-directory, I suppose. Maybe they're important.'

Tamsyn exploded. 'Well, if they're important,' she shouted in frustration, 'why haven't I seen their name in the newspapers?'

Almost as she said it, Tamsyn looked at Josh. As one, their eyes lit up as they realized what they could do next. They went for the mouse together. Josh just got there first.

Returning to the home page, he clicked on NET NAVIGATOR. The start menu came up.

'There!' shouted Tamsyn, pointing at one particular line. 'Try that one!'

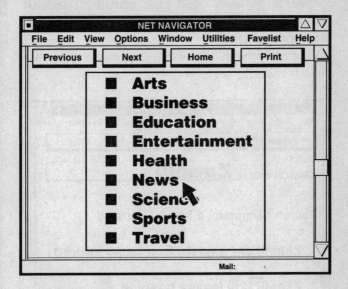

Josh clicked on it.

NEWS led to another menu which had FOR-EIGN, NATIONAL and LOCAL in it. Josh clicked on LOCAL. Another menu presented itself.

'Josh!' cried Tamsyn, pointing. At the bottom of the menu was an entry she hadn't noticed before: KEYWORD SEARCH. Josh clicked on it. Immediately a panel popped up:

SEARCH FOR:

Tamsyn leaned across and typed: ZANELLI . . . and waited.

'What's it doing?' she said after nothing had appeared for almost two minutes.

'Searching files?' said Josh, unsure. 'Loads of them, maybe. Depends on how far back they go with their archives.'

Just as Tamsyn was about to give up hope, the search ended.

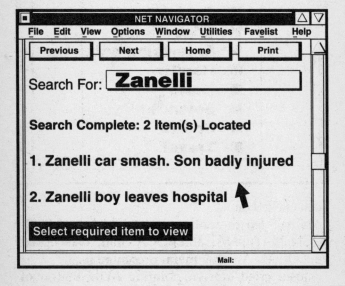

'Car smash?' said Tamsyn quietly. She and Josh looked at each other. Silently, he clicked the mouse button. After a short pause, the screen resolved into the display of a newspaper cutting. It was dated 5th May, five years previously:

ZANELLI
CAR SMASH
══ Son Badly Injured ══

The son of prominent local business couple Paul Zanelli, 39, and Theresa Zanelli, 37, was badly injured when the car they were driving was hit by a runaway lorry yesterday afternoon on the notorious Eastern Road, after the driver lost control of his vehicle.

Eight-year-old Rob Zanelli, who was sitting in the rear seat of the car and took the full force of the collision, was rushed to hospital with serious injuries to his back and legs. He underwent an emergency operation last night.

A spokesman at the hospital issued a very brief bulletin: 'Rob's condition remains serious. He has multiple injuries to his spine, and is at present unable to use his legs. It is too early to say whether this condition is permanent.'

Mail:

'Rob Zanelli,' whispered Tamsyn.

They read the rest of the article in silence, almost forgetting why they'd been searching for it in the first place. Finally, Tamsyn clicked on the second of the two articles their search had found. This was dated October, five months after the other one:

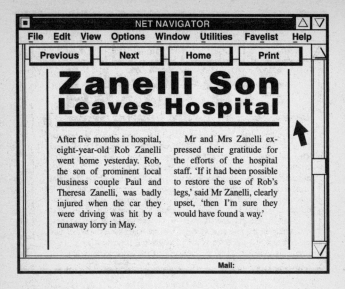

Zanelli Son Leaves Hospital

After five months in hospital, eight-year-old Rob Zanelli went home yesterday. Rob, the son of prominent local business couple Paul and Theresa Zanelli, was badly injured when the car they were driving was hit by a runaway lorry in May.

Mr and Mrs Zanelli expressed their gratitude for the efforts of the hospital staff. 'If it had been possible to restore the use of Rob's legs,' said Mr Zanelli, clearly upset, 'then I'm sure they would have found a way.'

Mail:

Tamsyn stood up and gazed out of the Technology Block window. *Paralysed*, she thought. How awful. Could that be something to do with why he needed help?

'Josh, we've got to do something!' she shouted.

Josh looked as helpless as she felt. 'Tamsyn, be sensible. What *can* we do? We don't know where he lives.'

'We could ring the police. Tell them what we know. They'd be able to find him, wouldn't they.'

'Ring the police?' Josh raised an eyebrow. 'And tell them what? Tamsyn, we don't actually *know* anything.'

Tamsyn flopped back on her chair. Josh was right, she knew that. But simply doing nothing . . .

She looked at the Internet screen. Why hadn't

Lauren King replied? She'd obviously believed her note enough to send it on to the others, but she hadn't answered herself.

Why ever not?

Toronto, Canada.
10.50 a.m. (UK time 3.50 p.m.)

'Allie, it must be here *somewhere!*' yelled Lauren.

Again she slid a diskette into the drive of their computer and scanned the list of files on it. Nothing. The file she was looking for just wasn't there.

'Have you tried them all?' said her grandmother.

'A dozen times!' Lauren pulled the last disk from the plastic box on her lap. 'I'm going to try this one once more. If it's not on here, then that file of Rob's has gone.'

Switching diskettes, she again clicked on the A: drive icon of her file manager program. The list of files came up. Lauren shook her head.

'It isn't there. It isn't on any of these, Allie. I've tried all ten of these disks, and it isn't on any of them!'

Ten?

Taking the diskette from the drive and putting it back into the box, Lauren counted. '. . . eight, nine. There's one missing.'

'You sure?' said Alice, leaning over to look for herself.

'Yes. There were ten disks in this box.'

Her grandmother's sudden movement made

Lauren look up. 'Allie . . .' she began – but her grandmother was already on her way out of the room.

A few clatters and bangs later she was back again, carrying a drawer from the kitchen cabinet. As Lauren looked on amazed, Alice emptied it on to the lounge carpet.

'There might . . . just might,' said Alice, '. . . be one in here.'

'In there?' shouted Lauren. 'Allie, you're supposed to look after disks. Keep them clean and dust-free. I mean . . .'

She was interrupted by Alice's triumphant shout of *'A-ha!'* Moments later she'd fished out a disk from the middle of the pile. It had bits of sticky tape and a number of unidentifiable stains on its black casing.

'What's it doing in there?' cried Lauren, taking it from her.

Alice looked unrepentant. 'I found some very nice recipes on the Internet. So I thought, *I'll save them*. And I did. On that disk.'

'But why put it in *that* drawer?'

Alice lifted a cookbook from the heap of junk. 'Because it's my recipes drawer, of course! Now, are you going to try it or not?'

Dusting the disk off as best she could, and hoping that it wouldn't gum up their drive, Lauren pushed it home. Again she scanned the file list. And there it was – ZMASTER.BMP – the file she'd been looking for.

She began to type a message to Tamsyn . . .

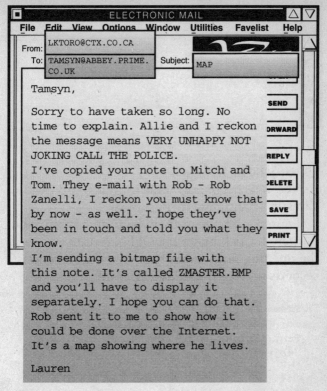

ELECTRONIC MAIL

File Edit View Options Window Utilities Favelist Help

From: LKTORO@CTX.CO.CA

To: TAMSYN@ABBEY.PRIME.CO.UK   Subject: MAP

SEND

ORWARD

REPLY

DELETE

SAVE

PRINT

Tamsyn,

Sorry to have taken so long. No
time to explain. Allie and I reckon
the message means VERY UNHAPPY NOT
JOKING CALL THE POLICE.
I've copied your note to Mitch and
Tom. They e-mail with Rob - Rob
Zanelli, I reckon you must know that
by now - as well. I hope they've
been in touch and told you what they
know.
I'm sending a bitmap file with
this note. It's called ZMASTER.BMP
and you'll have to display it
separately. I hope you can do that.
Rob sent it to me to show how it
could be done over the Internet.
It's a map showing where he lives.

Lauren

Lauren came out of the e-mail package and
clicked on another icon marked FILE TRANS-
FER. As the program asked for them, she quickly
typed in the name of the file, followed by
Tamsyn's user ID as the person to send it to.

The disk drive chugged and whirred for a few
seconds, its green light glowing. Then it flicked
off. Lauren sat back and sighed. The map was on
its way. She'd done all she could.

'Tamsyn,' she whispered, 'the rest is up to you.'

CHAPTER 9

Abbey School. 3.56 p.m.

As the two beeps sounded in quick succession, Tamsyn's hand flew to the mouse.

'Lauren – let one of them be from Lauren,' she muttered. Clicking on the OPEN button, she saw the opening lines of the header. It had taken just seconds to cross the Atlantic Ocean!

```
From: LKTORO@CTX.CO.CA
To: TAMSYN@ABBEY.PRIME.CO.UK
Sent: Friday 24 October at 10:55
Subject: MAP
```

'At last,' she breathed. Josh looked over her shoulder as they read down to the bottom of Lauren's note.

'What's a bitmap file?' said Tamsyn.

'Ah, now you're talking my language,' said Josh. 'It's a file with a picture in it. Budge up.'

Quickly, Josh came out of the mail package and into the file manager. A file called ZMASTER.BMP was waiting, just as Lauren had said.

With another couple of keystrokes, Josh had downloaded the file and entered a graphics package to display it.

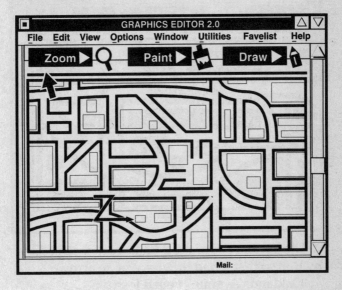

'That narrows it down,' said Josh, as they gazed at the screen, 'but it's still a big area.'

'Lauren said it shows where Rob lives,' said Tamsyn. 'It must be in the region of that letter Z.' She put her face close to the screen. 'What we could do with is a magnifying glass!'

'One magnifying glass coming up,' said Josh.

Sweeping the mouse pointer across to the letter Z, he double-clicked. Immediately, the centre of the map increased in size.

'Zoom function,' said Josh, double-clicking again to increase the map size yet more.

'Look!' yelled Tamsyn. 'Look at it!'

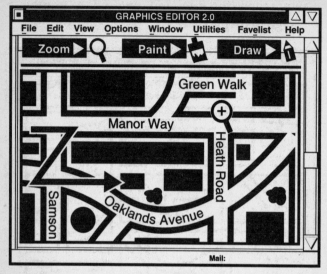

The bottom bar of the Z had clearly been edited by Rob so that it had the shape of an arrow.

'Oaklands Avenue!' yelled Josh.

Tamsyn was already on her feet. 'Come on, let's go!'

'Hang on,' said Josh. 'Shouldn't we call the police? If that's what he wants us to do.'

'Josh, it'll take for ever explaining everything to them! On our bikes we can get there in half the time. So, come on!'

Manor House. 4.15 p.m.
The hissing sound stopped.

Even from the lounge he'd been able to hear

it, imagining the sharp pointed flame of the oxyacetylene torch cutting a circle around the heavy combination lock.

As Rob had hoped, it had taken a long time. He remembered his father mentioning that the safe was a lot like their house: old and strong.

Rob tensed, listening for any further noises that might tell him what was happening. Opposite him, on the sofa where she'd been sitting ever since she'd brought him back from the study, Elaine Kirk didn't move – until footsteps sounded on the wooden floor of the hallway.

Then she stood up nervously.

'Brett? Have you found it?' Elaine said as the door was thrust open. Brett Hicks, his face smeared and sweating, came in.

Hicks didn't answer her. His eyes went straight for Rob.

'OK. Now I'm getting annoyed. Where is it? Where's that gold disk?'

Rob tried not to look as scared as he felt. 'I don't know! In the safe. You said it was in the safe.'

'Well, it's not!' With a sudden burst of anger, Hicks threw a handful of banknotes and papers across the floor. 'About a thousand quid and a bunch of insurance policies! That's the lot.'

Elaine Kirk dropped to her knees and began scrabbling for the notes. 'A thousand? Brett, let's take it. Let's go. Come on . . .'

'No!' Hicks glared at her. 'I want that disk,' he said quietly, menacingly. 'That disk is here. And I'm going to find it.'

Again, he turned to Rob. 'Where else could it be? Think, before I get really angry and do something I'll regret.'

As he said this, a look of fear crossed Elaine Kirk's face. 'Please, Brett. I didn't think it would be like this. Let's go.'

'We're going nowhere till I get that disk.' Clenching his fists, he moved closer to Rob. 'So think fast, kid. Where else could it be?'

Rob shook his head wildly. What could he say now? What could he do to play for more time?

'I told you. I don't know. I don't go in my dad's study. I've got my own room—'

He stopped, as if he'd just said something he regretted. Hicks picked up on it at once.

'Your room?' He looked at Elaine Kirk. 'You ever see his father go into his room?'

The tutor nodded. 'Of course. As soon as he comes home in the evening, before he goes out in the morning.' She gestured towards Rob. 'They both do, him and Mrs Zanelli.'

Hicks scowled at her. 'This morning. Was he in there this morning?'

Elaine Kirk nodded. 'Yes. Yes, I'm sure he was. He came out when I arrived.'

'And you never thought to mention that?' shouted Hicks. 'That disk could have been sitting in the kid's room all this time!'

Elaine Kirk shrank back as he stepped towards her, his hand raised. Then, without a word, he slammed the door and strode down the hallway towards Rob's room. Elaine was shaking with fear.

Rob closed his eyes in despair. It could only be a matter of time, now. Hicks would soon turn his room over.

Then he'd be back.

Portsmouth. 4.15 p.m.

The Portsmouth traffic was building up as the afternoon rush to leave the city began. Ignoring all she'd ever been taught about cycling safety, Tamsyn dodged on and off the pavement to make quicker progress.

Behind her, Josh was doing his best to keep up.

'We can get on a cycle lane that way,' Tamsyn shouted as she came to a junction she knew. 'It'll be quicker.'

Swinging off into a side road, Josh saw that Tamsyn was right. The solid white line of the bicycle lane stretched off into the distance. Soon they'd reached the busy Hilsea Roundabout.

'Not far now!' shouted Tamsyn. 'Just up to the top of Portsdown Hill.'

'I'll never make it!' gasped Josh.

'You're not fit!' Tamsyn called over her shoulder. Changing gears she stepped hard on the pedals as they followed the main A3 road as it snaked upwards.

By the time they reached the top of the hill, Tamsyn was out of breath too. 'Oaklands Avenue,' she gasped as Josh brought his bike to a halt. 'We're here.'

They looked around. Oaklands Avenue was tree-lined, and each of the houses seemed to be well shielded from the road by a thick hedge. The house nearest to them had iron gates, behind which was a neat and tidy gravel driveway.

'That isn't the one,' said Tamsyn briskly.

Josh looked at her. 'How do you know it isn't?' he said.

'Because it's got a gravel drive of course!'

'What?' Josh shook his head. 'A gravel drive? What's that got to do with anything?'

'Everything, of course! Pushing a wheelchair up a gravel drive would be murder! Josh, there'll be a house down here that's been altered to suit a wheelchair. It'll have smooth paths, and ramps instead of steps. I'll bet my life on it.'

She hurried on down the road. 'All we've got to do is find it. Find it quickly . . .'

Manor House. 4.29 p.m.

The noises coming from the direction of Rob's room left him in no doubt about what was going on. Hicks was turning out every cupboard, every cabinet. He was looking everywhere – through Rob's diskette boxes, on his shelves . . . under his bed . . .

'Rob . . .'

It was no more than a whisper. Elaine Kirk was looking at him, helplessly.

'I . . . I'm sorry,' was all she could manage.

Rob looked at her, wondering how she'd ever

got mixed up with somebody like Hicks.

Another loud clatter came from Rob's room, then the slam of the door. Elaine Kirk looked up as she realized Hicks was coming back.

'He must have found it,' she breathed.

But Rob wasn't listening. Nor, as Hicks came into the lounge, was Rob worrying about whether he'd found the gold diskette or not.

He was thinking, thinking furiously, about what to do when the two kids he'd just seen coming up the drive rang the doorbell.

4.33 p.m.
'Are you sure this is it?' said Josh, looking up at the front of the house.

'No,' said Tamsyn. 'But it looks the best bet, doesn't it?'

They'd spotted it as they'd walked back along Oaklands Avenue. A sign on the gatepost had read Manor House.

What was more, the house had fitted what she expected. The front doorway looked wider than most. The paths and driveway were all smooth tarmac. And, leading up to the front door was a ramp . . .

Surely it *had* to be the place.

Now, as they reached the front door of Manor House, Tamsyn hesitated. What if this was all a dreadful mistake? Shouldn't they simply run off before making fools of themselves?

Her finger hovered over the bellpush. It was

mounted on the wall at the side of the front door, above what looked like a small loudspeaker.

And then, with a determined jab, she pressed it.

CHAPTER 10

Manor House. 4.34 p.m.

The rasp of the bell seemed to cut through the air like a knife.

Inside the house there was total silence for a second. Elaine Kirk looked up, her eyes narrowed and questioning. Hicks stopped dead.

Only Rob was prepared for it. Easing his wheelchair backwards, he pushed himself closer to the wall.

'Who is it?' Hicks rasped at Elaine Kirk. 'Are you expecting anyone?'

Elaine shook her head. 'Nobody. Not at this time.' She got to her feet. 'Do you want me to answer it?'

Hicks looked at her. 'No! Leave it!' he said sharply.

The two of them waited, saying nothing. Slowly, Rob inched his way further back towards the wall.

The bell rang again, the sound hanging in the air. Hicks moved to the lounge door and peered out. From there, Rob knew, he'd be able to see through the glazed panel in the front door but not be seen himself.

'Two kids,' said Hicks at once. 'What do they want?' This time he spun round to look at Rob. 'School friends of yours?'

Rob shook his head. 'I don't go to school, remember.'

The bell sounded for a third time, a long harsh ring as if the callers at the door had decided to give it just one more try.

Hicks looked out into the hallway again. 'They're going,' he growled.

It was the chance Rob needed, the chance he'd hoped for. As Hicks looked away, Rob thrust his hand out. Close to the wall as he was, he could reach it now.

Pressing hard, Rob pushed the security button to open the front door.

Tamsyn heard the buzzer just as she stepped away from the front door. For a moment she wondered what it was. Then, looking round, she saw the speaker on the wall again and realized what had happened: without bothering to ask who was there, somebody inside the house had released the door catch.

Gingerly, she pushed against the solid front door. It opened with a gentle click.

'What are you doing?' whispered Josh. 'You can't just go in there!

Tamsyn was holding the door just tightly enough to stop it swinging closed again. 'Why not?' she said. 'He's just opened it for us.'

'You don't know what you'll find in there!' Josh was looking at her wild-eyed. 'You can't walk into strange houses on your own!'

'I'm not on my own. You're with me.'

'Yeah, but . . .'

'No buts, Josh. Come on.'

Tamsyn pushed through the front door and into the polished hallway . . .

'What the . . .'

As they came face to face with Brett Hicks, Tamsyn and Josh stopped dead. Whoever this guy was, he didn't look pleased to see them.

'Excuse me,' said Tamsyn, thinking at once how pathetic it sounded.

'Get out!' said Hicks.

Tamsyn automatically backed away. Behind her she could feel that Josh had done the same.

'Look . . . we—' began Tamsyn.

'I said, get out!' yelled Hicks again. This time he took a threatening step towards her.

'Sure.'

At the sound of Josh's voice, Tamsyn looked round. She'd expected to see him backing out through the front door and was surprised to see that he was actually moving away from the angry man, but further into the hallway.

'Now!' snarled Hicks.

'Yeah, yeah. Right.' Josh was still circling. 'It's just that . . .' he glanced towards Tamsyn and then back to the man, '. . . we thought you wanted to see us.'

'What?' said Hicks.

'I mean,' said Josh, 'this is the Zanelli residence, isn't it?'

The moment Josh said this, the man's anger seemed to fade. It looked to Tamsyn as if he didn't quite know what to say.

'It is, isn't it?' persisted Josh. 'The Zanelli house?'

'So? What if it is?' grunted Hicks.

'We got a message, see?' said Josh. 'Asking us to call round.'

'Message?'

'Yes, a message. From – Rob.'

Tamsyn saw the man's eyes flicker. Who was he? There was one way to find out. She said, 'Rob. Your son . . . is that right, er . . . Mr Zanelli?'

The man broke into a smile of sorts. 'Er . . . Yeah. Yeah, that's right. Well . . . so my boy Rob asked you to call round, did he? Sorry, he didn't say. Kids, huh?'

Josh laughed. 'Can we . . . er . . . say hello to him, then? Now we're here.'

'See him?'

'Yes, please,' said Tamsyn firmly.

Something was going on, she was certain of that, now. Whoever this guy was, with his gelled hair and sweating face, he wasn't Mr Zanelli. She'd just realized – he *couldn't* be Mr Zanelli. The newspaper report they'd found through the Internet had said that Mr Zanelli was 39 years old at the time of the accident. He would be 44 now, and there was no way this man could be anything like that age!

Then the man stunned her. Looking back towards the lounge door, he said, 'No problem. I'll just get him for you.'

Leaving Tamsyn and Josh in the hallway, Hicks stepped into the lounge and closed the door. He stepped straight across to Rob and grabbed him fiercely by the arm.

'Now listen. Listen good. There's two of your mates out there. You're going to go out there with me, and pretend I'm your father. Understand?' His grip on Rob tightened. 'Get rid of them. Because if you don't, you'll regret it.'

He bent low, his gaze boring into Rob. 'You got that?'

Rob nodded.

Hicks went behind his wheelchair and pushed Rob slowly forward. Elaine Kirk was still sitting, motionless, on the sofa. 'You, stay there!' he barked.

In the hallway, Tamsyn and Josh saw the lounge door begin to open. What were they going to do now? What were they going to say?

Rob made the decision for them. Before they could open their mouths, he was greeting them as if they were old friends.

'Tamsyn! Thanks for coming round!'

Tamsyn simply smiled and nodded. 'Hi . . . er . . . Rob. This is Josh.'

Josh nodded. 'Hi. Tamsyn's told me all about

you. What can we . . . er . . . do for you?'

Rob spoke again. 'Look, I know it's a pain but . . . could you both do me a favour? I've got an old dot-matrix printer I don't use any more. I know Abbey School's into computing. Could you find a home for it?'

'Er . . . sure,' mumbled Josh.

Tamsyn exchanged glances with him. What was going on?

'I'd sort it out myself but, y'know . . .' Rob patted the side of his wheelchair, '. . . it's tricky.'

Tamsyn looked at Rob. Something told her that this was a boy who could do *anything* if he wanted to.

'Of course – Rob,' she said.

'Thanks,' said Rob. He looked up at Brett Hicks. 'Could you get it for them . . . Dad?'

Hicks nodded, smiling.

'It's in the cupboard, Dad,' said Rob. 'That one,' he added, pointing at one of the many doors around the wide hallway.

Tamsyn was totally confused. What was going on? As the man strode across the polished floor, she stole a glance at Rob – to see him extend the fingers of both hands and put them together to form a sideways 'L' shape.

The negative sign! The door he'd sent the man towards was *not* a cupboard! Then what was it? Tamsyn tensed, ready to do whatever she had to.

It was just as well she did, because what happened next took place in a bewildering blur. To Rob, though, it seemed more like slow motion, so anxious was he that his plan should succeed.

Hicks was heading straight for the door. Slowly, Rob slid his fingers down onto the hand-rails mounted on the wheels of his chair.

Not yet . . . he told himself . . . *not yet . . . now!*

As Hicks swung open the door, Rob pushed down on his wheels with all his might. Accelerating quickly, he hurtled forward.

Already Hicks was turning round, realizing he'd been tricked. Behind him, as Tamsyn could now see, wasn't the inside of a cupboard but the top of a flight of stairs. That was what Rob had been telling her. The doorway Rob had sent him to led down into the Manor House cellar.

'Aaaah!'

Rob slammed into Hicks with all the force he could muster. As Hicks toppled backwards, he tried to clutch the door frame for support but his fingers slipped. He stumbled down the top couple of steps. Grabbing hold of a handrail, he stopped himself falling any further. With blazing eyes, he started back up again.

Frantically, Rob reversed and slammed the cellar door shut. 'Help me!' he cried. 'Help me!'

Already prepared, though not knowing for what, Tamsyn raced across the hallway. She slammed herself against the door just as Hicks hurled himself against it from the other side. The door bounced open by a fraction, then slammed shut again as Josh leapt forward and hit it like a rugby player.

Behind the door, though, Hicks was finding

extra strength in his desperation. Again the door bounced open.

'We can't hold it!' shouted Josh.

Suddenly, they heard the sound of clattering heels. Moments later, another pair of hands was helping them. As the cellar door was slammed shut, Rob leaned forward and turned the key in the lock.

'Elaine?' he said.

His tutor looked down at him for a moment, tears in her eyes. Then, looking around her like a frightened animal, she suddenly made a dash for the front door.

'What on earth's going on?' yelled Tamsyn.

'Tell you later,' shouted Rob. 'Stop her!'

Tamsyn didn't think twice. Racing across the polished floor, she got to the smart-looking woman just as she was trying to wrench open the front door. Breaking free, Elaine Kirk spun away.

Then, as if she couldn't think of anything else, Elaine Kirk made her second dash for the front door. This time, Tamsyn's feet slipped on the polished floor. In an instant the woman was past her. Throwing open the front door, she ran out ... and stopped, as the strong voice of the real Mr Zanelli said:

'Elaine. Sorry to mess you about. We managed to get away after all ...'

As she saw Mr and Mrs Zanelli standing on the doorstep, Elaine Kirk turned back into the hallway.

This time, Tamsyn made no mistake. As the tutor ran, she thrust out her leg. Elaine Kirk went flying, sliding across the polished floor to end up on her back. Quickly, Tamsyn ran across to grab her by the arms while Josh stood guard.

'They were looking for the *Lure of the Labyrinth* diskette,' blurted out Rob. 'She let him in as soon as you'd gone. They've been here all day, turning the place over!'

Mrs Zanelli held up a hand. 'Whoa, whoa. What's been going on? Who's been here?'

A sudden pounding and shouting came from behind the cellar door. 'And who is in there?'

'Brett Hicks.'

'Hicks?' said Mr Zanelli, glancing towards the locked door. 'Not . . .'

'Yes. The Brett Hicks you sacked for trying to hack into the development computer,' said Rob.

With a few quick strides, Mr Zanelli went down to his study. Moments later he was telephoning for the police. A patrol car was screeching up the drive in minutes.

Rob explained quickly what had been going on. Elaine Kirk nodded dumbly at every statement.

'She did help us shut Hicks in,' said Rob, when he'd finished.

At the command of the policeman in charge the cellar door was opened, and a pair of handcuffs was snapped on to Brett Hicks's wrists the moment he came out.

As he was being led away, Mr Zanelli stepped in front of him. 'Can you search him first?' he asked the policeman in charge. 'He could have a valuable computer disk on him.'

'Come off it, Zanelli,' snarled Hicks. 'Who are you trying to kid? After some insurance money, are you? That disk's not here.'

Mr Zanelli looked at the officer. 'It is here. I left it here this morning.'

'It can't be!' shouted Hicks. 'I turned this whole place over.'

'It is here,' Rob said quietly.

As all eyes turned to him, he slipped his hand down the side of his wheelchair – and pulled out the *Lure of the Labyrinth* disk.

Mr Zanelli looked as if he didn't know whether to laugh or cheer as he reached out to take it.

'It may be a bit warm, Dad,' said Rob. 'I've been sitting on it all day!'

As Elaine Kirk and Brett Hicks were led away, Mr and Mrs Zanelli turned to Rob. 'You're sure you're all right?' Mr Zanelli asked. 'If that thug hurt you . . .'

Rob shook his head. 'Dad, I'm fine.' He looked at Tamsyn and Josh. 'I might not have been, though. Tamsyn and Josh got here just in time.'

'Rob sent us a note over the Internet,' said Tamsyn. She smiled at Rob. 'Well, a sort of note . . .'

Step by step, they took Mr and Mrs Zanelli through what had happened from the moment they first received Rob's coded message to their arrival at the house.

'But how did you get in?' asked Mrs Zanelli.

'The door control panel in the lounge,' said Rob. 'I saw them coming up the drive . . . so I opened the door for them!'

'You've been very brave,' said Mr Zanelli. His voice was a mix of pride and relief.

'So were these two,' said Rob, indicating Tamsyn and Josh. 'When they did come in, Hicks did his best to scare them off. I'm surprised they didn't run for it.'

'I was ready to,' said Tamsyn. 'If Josh hadn't stayed . . .' She turned to Josh. 'Now I come to think of it . . . why *did* you stay? You were the one who was telling me all along that Rob's message was a joke.'

Josh shrugged modestly. 'It was Hicks. When he started blasting off at us I realized it was for real.'

'I don't follow,' said Rob.

'Simple. He was yelling at us to go – and yet

the door had been opened for us. It hadn't been opened by him, so it had to have been opened by somebody else – somebody who *didn't* want us to go!' He grinned at Rob. 'And that had to be you!'

Mrs Zanelli took their hands in hers. 'Well, we want to thank you both.' Tamsyn smiled. Josh went a deep shade of pink. 'Where did you come from?'

'Abbey School,' said Josh, thankful for the chance to get his hand back. 'It's about four miles from here. In the city.'

'Just a little bike ride,' laughed Tamsyn, winking at Josh.

'Good school, is it?' asked Mr Zanelli.

Josh answered at once. 'Yeah. It's really good. The kids are friendly. Some of the teachers, even. There's clubs and stuff – like the Computer Club. And the new Technology Block is brilliant!'

Mr and Mrs Zanelli laughed. 'You obviously enjoy it there.'

'Yeah . . . well,' said Josh. 'If you've got to go to school, then . . . Abbey might as well be the one to go to.'

Mr and Mrs Zanelli looked at each other thoughtfully. 'Rob,' said Mr Zanelli, 'after Josh and Tamsyn have telephoned home to say where they are, why don't you show them your computer set-up? Your room's a mess, but at least our friend Hicks left that in one piece.'

Rob's dad was right. As Rob edged his wheelchair into the room he saw that, although Hicks had turned over everywhere else, his computer system was untouched.

'Wow!' said Josh, following it up with a whistle. 'All this gear is yours?'

Rob nodded, but his smile was forced. 'It helps make up for not being able to go to school,' he said softly. 'At least with this and the Internet I can meet other kids.'

'Like us,' said Tamsyn.

Rob looked at her. 'Abbey School sounds a good place.'

'It is,' said Tamsyn. 'There are hardly any dead people there at all! Even Mr Findlay's still breathing . . . I think!'

Rob held up his hands, grinning as he remembered his first e-mail to Tamsyn, asking if Abbey was as dead a place as it sounded. 'OK, OK. I apologize. I was only joking, you know.'

'I know,' said Tamsyn. 'I didn't know about smileys then.'

'But we sure do now!' exclaimed Josh. 'I mean, we aren't ever going to forget them, are we? But – why did you send your note that way? Why not just write out what you wanted to tell us?'

'No time,' said Rob. 'Besides, I didn't want Elaine spotting it.' He looked at Tamsyn and Josh in turn. 'Good job you were great at code busting!'

'It wasn't just us,' said Tamsyn. 'Tom, Lauren and Mitch did their bit as well.'

'A spot of international detection!' said Josh.

'More a case of Internet detection,' laughed Tamsyn.

A little while later, Josh got to his feet and said, 'Rob – I've got to be going. Y'know, homework and all that. But . . .' he tapped a loving hand on Rob's computer, 'can I come round again soon?'

'Can *we* come round again soon?' laughed Tamsyn, knowing what Josh was getting at.

Rob went ahead of them towards the hallway. 'Sure. Come any time. And don't forget to check your e-mail. You'll find a few more notes from the mysterious ZMASTER!'

As they reached the front door, Mr and Mrs Zanelli came up behind them.

'Rob,' began Mr Zanelli, 'your mother and I have just been talking.'

'About a new tutor,' continued Mrs Zanelli.

Rob looked up at them. 'What about a new tutor?'

'That, before we do anything about finding another one,' said Mr Zanelli, breaking into a smile, 'perhaps we should have a word with the headteacher at Abbey School first.'

'You mean—' Rob began to say.

'Of course he means it!' cried Josh. 'Mr Zanelli, Mrs Zanelli, that would be brilliant. I mean, at least if he comes to Abbey you'll know he's safe!'

'Josh is right,' said Tamsyn, delighted. 'We won't let Rob out of our sight.'

Rob looked up sharply. 'Hey, I'm not helpless you know. I just can't walk, that's all.'

Tamsyn returned his look, and more. Josh braced himself for the blast.

'I never said you were helpless!' Her face broke into a broad smile. 'We're just not going to let you out of sight until you've helped us write our Internet report for Mr Findlay!'

Manor House.
Wednesday 29 October, 6.05 p.m.
Rob typed excitedly, his fingers darting over the keyboard.

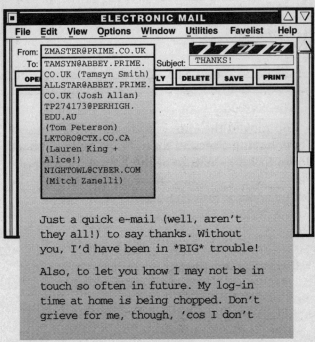

```
┌─────────────────────────────────────────────────────┐
│ ■        ELECTRONIC MAIL              △ ▽│
├─────────────────────────────────────────────────────┤
│ File  Edit  View  Options  Window  Utilities  Favelist  Help │
├─────────────────────────────────────────────────────┤
│ From:  ZMASTER@PRIME.CO.UK                           │
│ To:   TAMSYN@ABBEY.PRIME.  Subject: │ THANKS! │      │
│       CO.UK (Tamsyn Smith)                           │
│ OPEN  ALLSTAR@ABBEY.PRIME.  LY  DELETE  SAVE  PRINT  │
│       CO.UK (Josh Allan)                             │
│       TP274173@PERHIGH.                              │
│       EDU.AU                                         │
│       (Tom Peterson)                                 │
│       LKTORO@CTX.CO.CA                               │
│       (Lauren King +                                 │
│       Alice!)                                        │
│       NIGHTOWL@CYBER.COM                             │
│       (Mitch Zanelli)                                │
│                                                      │
│       Just a quick e-mail (well, aren't              │
│       they all!) to say thanks. Without              │
│       you, I'd have been in *BIG* trouble!           │
│                                                      │
│       Also, to let you know I may not be in          │
│       touch so often in future. My log-in            │
│       time at home is being chopped. Don't           │
│       grieve for me, though, 'cos I don't            │
└─────────────────────────────────────────────────────┘
```

```
mind. The reason is that I'll be
starting at Abbey School in a couple
of weeks!

I'll not be completely out of touch,
though. I'm told there's an excellent
Tech. Block just waiting to be used
properly. [Tamsyn and Josh: That was
a joke!] So between the six of us we
should be able to do some *real*
surfing!

Who knows, maybe there'll be some
other cases for the Internet
Detectives to crack!

ZMASTER
```

Mail:

Rob moved the cursor up to the SEND button.
Then, having a second thought, he moved it back
down to his signature at the bottom of his note.
There, before sending his note on its way, he
added another four characters.

:-))

It was just how he felt.